What's Life Without the Sprinkles?

by

Misty Simon

What's Life Without the Sprinkles?

Cover Art by *Debbie Taylor*

The Wild Rose Press, Inc.
PO Box 708
Adams Basin, NY 14410-0708
Visit us at www.thewildrosepress.com

Publishing History
First Champagne Rose Edition, 2013
Print ISBN 978-1-61217-653-6
Digital ISBN 978-1-61217-654-3

Published in the United States of America

She almost ran the stop sign at the corner of Broad and Keller because of a guy out in the front yard of the house to her left. He had his shirt up from the hem, wiping his forehead with the tag end of the white fabric. His strong forearms moved and tensed with the swiping motion, making the saliva all but dry up in Claudia's mouth.

She would bet that last check for eight thou that Edward did not look like that under his neatly pressed button-down shirt. This man was toned and lightly golden even now at the beginning of spring. His muscles contracted as he took one last swipe at his face, wiping right at his brow line. The sleeves of the white T-shirt hugged him like a second skin. His jeans rode low on his hips and were rimmed by a tool belt with a wrench and a drill. Was it dirty that she was drooling this hard over someone who was just doing his job?

Must be sweaty work, she thought as she continued to sit at the stop sign. Maybe she could offer him a drink of water, and perhaps she could fan him with the bank slip she'd just picked up. Lust came freight-training through her and she let it because this was a random guy she might not see again. And even if she was looking for safe in dating, that didn't mean she was dead.

In fact, she wouldn't mind licking some icing off that flat stomach. Whew, boy!

A horn beeped behind her, and she realized two things at once. She was still sitting at a stop sign with three cars behind her, and when the shirt came down from the guy's face, she saw it was Nate, waving at her.

Holy Mary, Mother of God, she was going to hell.

Praise for Misty Simon

"Misty Simon has a way of making me burst out in laughter one moment and tears in the next."
~Kim Robinson, BBW Reviews
"Ms. Simon is an astonishing writer."
~Book Reviews by Crystal blog
"This is definitely an author to watch out for and we can expect excellent works to come."
~Liadan, Coffee Time Romance
"Misty Simon's *A MOTHER'S HEART* is heart wrenchingly sweet…. A wonderful first book from a great new author."
~Valerie, Manic Readers
"I highly recommend this book for a great story… [It] should be on everyone's 'To be read' list. It's also a great look into animal rescue."
~Brenda Talley, The Romance Studio (5 Hearts)
"Ms. Simon has created a wonderful tale of sparkling characters."
~Hollie, Coffee Time Romance (4 Cups)
"If you enjoy romance stories about two people burned by relationships gone bad…then look no further."
~Xeranthemum, Long and Short Reviews (4.5 Books)
"A cute tale about a woman afraid to turn out like her mother and a man trying to take care of his children."
~Debbie Gould, WRDF Review
"*A MOTHER'S HEART* is a modern-day love story…. I…would like to read more by this author."
~Lily, Simply Romance Reviews
"Put together a pack of dogs, adorable kids and a yummy neighbor…an amusing tale!"
~Crystal, CK2s Kwips and Kritiques

Dedication

To my husband and daughter,
who know how to fold their own laundry
and make dinner if necessary.
You both make this fun and worth doing!
To Jason Manns,
who makes the music that makes my heart sing
and my fingers fly over the keyboard.
And to Elodia Eddy,
my first reader.
This was a long journey and thank you!

Chapter One

A hush, broken only by the ticking of the antique grandfather clock, fell over the crowd in the spacious room. When one of the three doors on the far wall slowly swung open, the crowd sucked in a collective breath. Within seconds, that collective inhale was released in tears and joyous laughter.

The dressing room of Decadence, the scene of this rite of passage, was filled with every shape and size of woman, seventeen total, gathered on this spring morning to approve their friend's wedding gown.

The mother of the bride raised her hand dramatically and another hush immediately ensued. Claudia Bradley had seen it so many times it was like a choreographed ocean wave. The noise swelled and receded, depending on the mother's whim, after the resplendent bride-to-be hesitantly stepped into the throng of women.

Standing alone on the edge of the crowd, Claudia watched as the mother cupped the daughter's face in her hands and kissed her on the cheek. Claudia's friend, May Blanchard, who had created the dress, winked at her and turned back to the bride.

Claudia discreetly took her leave and went to the bakery section of the store, where she was far more comfortable. Very few people cried over cake, unless it was her Double Deluxe Chocolate Fantasy with Butter

Cream Icing.

An hour later, after stamping the check from the mother of the bride For Deposit Only, Claudia ran back to the tiny office they all shared and grabbed up the phone. Hitting the first speed-dial number, she waited impatiently, dancing from one high-heeled foot to another. "Come on, come on," she said as the phone continued to ring in her ear. Finally, the line was answered, and Claudia didn't waste any time with pleasantries.

"You are talking to the proud new holder of an eight-thousand-dollar check," she crowed, still astounded. They had never been able to charge that much for a dress before. And there would be more where that came from, when the bridal party put in orders for the flowers and the cake.

"Holy cow," said her best friend, Nate West, his voice rife with disbelief.

"None holier."

"Hey, hang on, let me turn down the television."

Claudia smiled. Typical Nate. "No, no. Don't worry about it. I have to call Zoe anyway, so I have to go, but I just wanted to yell it at you first." Nothing had ever felt better.

"Well, that's awesome. We'll celebrate this weekend, if you don't have plans."

"You're on and you're buying." Before he could protest, she hung up and twirled around, almost knocking into the desk chair and the bookshelf.

Once she righted herself, she picked up the phone again and called her sister. She crowed the same few beautiful words, emphasizing the amount this time.

"Get out of here," her sister Zoe screamed.

"I am getting out. I have to go to the bank and cash this puppy, after I photocopy it to hang on our wall."

"Well, make sure it's in that tiny space we call an office, so we can charge even more next time. Why tie ourselves down by announcing that eight thousand dollars is a lot for us? Are they coming back for flowers next week? Did you remember to ask?"

"You are absolutely right," Claudia said, and laughed. "And yes, they are coming in, and I remembered to confirm. Thanks for all your support." *Eight thousand dollars.* And for a dress May had sewn over bowls of corn flakes and reruns of *Friends*. Outstanding.

Zoe's voice brought her back. "I can run it to the bank, if you want. I'll stop by between errands."

Claudia laughed again. "Yeah, you wish. I got it covered, and I won't be tempted to go buy a new wardrobe."

Zoe, as usual, ignored her. "So what's the first thing you're going to do with your vast portion of the money?"

"I'm going to find a boarding school to tuck Justin into until he stops leaving his clothes all over the floor, wanting a dog, and tracking mud in the house. Oh, and dropping hints that it would be a good idea if I found a man." Boarding school wasn't a bad idea, but not one she'd follow through on. She'd miss her son too much, but God, he was giving her fits lately, constantly asking about her love life.

"You wouldn't really do that, and you know it. He may be a pain right now, but you would freak if he was more than ten miles away."

Claudia sighed. "How true."

"So what are you really doing to celebrate?"

"Nothing really. Get back to work, I guess."

"You're killing me, Claudia. Mom said she's taking Justin for the night, so I know you have a whole night to yourself and you have no other plans? What kind of life is that?"

A safe one, Claudia thought, but said, "I do have plans. I'm going out with Edward." Then she cringed—on her end of the phone, where Zoe couldn't possibly see her.

"God save me from dear old Eddie." Zoe's sarcasm came across the line loud and clear. "Oh, pardon me, it's not Eddie or Ed, but Edward. Didn't he say it sounded more dignified? Sounds to me like he has a stick up his..."

Claudia broke in before this spiraled into a conversation where Zoe used all the swear words her first boyfriend had ever taught her. "Please don't start. It's a date. I'm doing something other than staying home and drinking margaritas alone. You should be happy."

"I would be," Zoe said, exasperation evident in her tone, "if it was anyone but that pony. Remember our little talk about stabling the pony and harnessing a stallion? What happened to the resolve to drop this dork and find someone worthy of your time?"

"He's not a dork. He's a very nice man our mother introduced me to." That was her story and she was sticking to it.

"He's a pony."

"He is not a pony. We have a very good time together."

"I can tell, since you always get so formal

whenever you talk about him." Zoe's breath came out in a huff over the line. "Look, if the pony/stallion scenario isn't working for you, then maybe this one will…"

Claudia held her breath, not sure what her sister would come up with next.

"Let's say Edward is a dessert."

Claudia groaned.

"Bear with me. So if I had to pick Edward out of a dessert case, I would say he was the three-day-old cookies on the clearance rack at the grocery store."

"That's not fair."

"Regardless, he *is* stale cookies, and what you need is cake. Preferably cake with butter cream icing in the swirly patterns I love to watch you do, Claudia. Lots of cake, with sugar and excitement. When are you going to ignore Mom and her ridiculous matchmaking and go out and grab some delicious cake? Find someone worthy of your time?"

A pause hummed along the line. Claudia squeezed her eyes shut and hoped Zoe wouldn't say it. So, of course, she did.

"Someone like Nate, maybe."

Argh!

"Don't start. I'm happy with Edward." It was only a tiny white lie. While he might not be cake, she wasn't willing to call him three-day-old stale cookies from the grocery store, either. That wasn't fair to him or the relationship she had been trying hard to cultivate over the last three months. She tuned back to the conversation before she could look too hard at the fact that the relationship with him was already work and they hadn't even slept together yet.

"The day I see you truly be happy with Eddie is the day I turn my hair green," Zoe said, then added, "on purpose. That botched bleach job doesn't count. And I still think you should go jump on Nate."

The bell above the door tinkled, Gratefully, Claudia looked up to see one of the women from the earlier bridal crowd walk back into the shop. "I have to go," she whispered. "Customer." Without a moment's hesitation, she hung up on Zoe's continued slamming of Edward's character and possible toupee. Her comments about cake weren't helping, either. Claudia had been on a steady diet of no sweets for over ten years. There was no need to introduce them now, especially not with Nate, her best friend.

****

After dropping off the check at their bank and grabbing some lunch, Claudia took a drive around town. She had nothing else going on today in the shop, and May had everything under control. If she needed Claudia, May would call and Claudia could be back in moments, such was the joy of a small town.

With the windows rolled down, she enjoyed the light breeze of mid-April in Central Pennsylvania. It was one of her favorite times of year. Plants and trees were in bloom, animals were coming back to life after sleeping away the winter, and summer was just around the corner.

In fact, today felt more like summer than spring. Claudia enjoyed the way the sun beat into the car and the warmth on her elbow where she had it cocked out the window. Tunes played on the radio, no one was bugging her about her love life, her child wasn't giving her fits with pre-teen angst, and her sister wasn't plaguing her with things she couldn't have and didn't want. Not much could go wrong right now.

And even though she was not looking forward to dinner with Edward tonight as much as she had before her talk with Zoe and her ridiculous cake references, she would get her enthusiasm back any minute now. In the meantime, she drove past the high school and then past the elementary school building where Justin was hopefully learning and not getting into any trouble.

"Eleven o'clock and all is well," Claudia said to herself.

Seconds later, though, she almost ran the stop sign at the corner of Broad and Keller because of a guy out in the front yard of the house to her left. He was maybe ten yards back from the street, his booted feet planted next to a bucket of paint and a ladder to the second floor where apparently the window frames were being repainted. But the paint didn't hold her attention for long, since the abs on the guy taking a break from the painting were about all she could truly focus on.

He had his shirt up from the hem, wiping his forehead with the tag end of the white fabric. His strong forearms moved and tensed with the swiping motion, making the saliva all but dry up in Claudia's mouth. She would bet that last check for eight thou that Edward did not look like that under his neatly pressed button-down shirt. This man was toned and lightly golden even at the beginning of spring. His muscles contracted as he took one last swipe at his face, wiping right at his brow line. The sleeves of the white T-shirt hugged him like a second skin. His jeans rode low on his hips and were rimmed by a tool belt with a wrench and a drill. Was it dirty that she was drooling this hard over someone who was just doing his job?

Must be sweaty work, she thought as she continued to sit at the stop sign. Maybe she could offer him a drink of water, and perhaps she could fan him with the bank slip she'd just picked up. Lust came freight-training through her, and she let it because this was a random guy she might not see again. And even if she was looking for safe in dating, that didn't mean she was dead.

In fact, she wouldn't mind licking some icing off that flat stomach. Whew, boy!

A horn beeped behind her, and she realized two things at once. She was still sitting at a stop sign with three cars behind her, and when the shirt came down from the guy's face, she saw it was Nate, waving at her.

Holy Mary, Mother of God, she was going to hell. And it was all Zoe's fault.

****

"I have a schedule to keep today, Logan," Nate West said as his younger brother walked up the sidewalk through the late morning sunshine. Claudia had just driven by, and he'd waved to her, but she had looked stressed. He made a mental note to give her a call later to see what was going on now in her often chaotic life. The phone call about the check had been brief, and then he'd had to leave for an appointment. He'd gotten some work done ahead of Logan's arrival and planned on doing more after he left with the specs.

"Yeah, yeah, keep your shorts on. I'm only five minutes late, bro."

"Well, that's five minutes I could have been doing something else. And the sun is only getting higher." Nate walked along the outside of the Victorian house.

They needed to get the specs to make a bid for the rest of the job. Right now they were proving themselves to Old Mrs. Finkey by painting the windows, but she wanted the whole thing remodeled. Nate definitely wanted to be the one to have his hands on this old beauty. The architecture was awesome, and the job challenging enough to make his fingers itch to get at it.

"So what did the old man say about this job?"

"He's going to give us the material costs when he gets back to the office, but for right now we just need to look around and see how much work the house is going to need." This was one of the aspects of construction Nate loved. Taking something old and making it new. That was what had drawn him to the family business in the first place. Sure, it was nice to build from the ground up, but it was better to remake and strengthen.

They spent about thirty minutes going over the various repairs and build-outs needed to give Mrs. Finkey what she wanted.

Taking one more turn around the property, Nate knew they could do this and probably come in under budget. He could even work it in around the repairs they were doing on Decadence for Claudia and her partners. It would be a nice boost to his checking account at the same time, too.

"I don't see why we couldn't do it," Logan said, running a hand along the siding. "It should fit right in with what we're doing at your girlfriend's place."

Nate caught the sideways sly look and the gleam in his brother's eye. But he wasn't going to rise to the bait. No way. "I don't see why not, either."

"Unless you have to watch Justin again so Claudia can go out and make time with another man while you sit at home, playing games with the kid and trying not to think about her sleeping with someone else."

Nate tried to ignore the jab again, but he was nearing the end of his rope. "Just let it go."

"Well, I'd love to, but it pains me to see you moping around all the time."

"I do not mope, you ass. She and I are friends, have been friends, for years. I don't know why you obsess about what she's doing and who she's doing it with. And I happen to like the kid, and so do you."

Logan ignored all but what he thought was important. "Yes, you do mope. You moon around after her, doing everything for her..."

Whatever else Logan said was lost in the roar filling Nate's head. His eyes couldn't believe what he was seeing cruising along the road. It was like being thrown back over ten years to high school. Radio cranked up, windows down, top lowered on the vintage Mustang he'd driven all those years ago, Peter Drake breezed through town as if he owned it.

Shit.

"Hey, have you heard anything I've said?" Logan said, tapping Nate on the shoulder.

"What?" What the hell was Peter Drake doing back in town? He should have been tucked up in Ohio, not glooming up the skyline in Pennsylvania.

"I was telling you you're being an idiot with Claudia."

"Whatever. I have bigger things to worry about right now."

"Well, that's certainly a different tune for you. Normally, you obsess about her."

Nate dragged himself back from wondering about

Peter and hit Logan in the arm. "Don't worry about it. We'll put the bid in with Dad and go from there. I have something to do that can't wait."

"But what about the other two jobs?" Logan scratched his head, then crossed his arms.

"I don't have time for this. There's something I have to do."

****

"Emergency girl meeting."

Claudia opened her mouth to tell May she couldn't possibly leave what she was doing, as the other woman breezed past. She'd just gotten back from her ill-fated car ride and needed to do some serious decorating to distract herself from the image of Nate with his shirt half off. She'd already ignored three calls from him on her cell. She couldn't talk to him until she figured out a way to not picture him as she'd seen him near the stop sign. And the thought struck her that he was going to be working on Decadence in that capacity, too. She hoped she and her sanity survived.

In the meantime, May was yelling her name from the back office. Okay. She finished piping the icing around the edges of the top layer of the three-tiered cake for tomorrow afternoon's senior tea and set down the white plastic bag. After washing her hands, she ducked into the back room and found Zoe already there. Why did everything seem to be such a crisis lately? She didn't think she could take another one.

"What's going on that you had to interrupt everything?" Zoe asked the question before Claudia could get it out.

"Claudia, I have something I have to tell you, and you're not going to like it." May took the seat behind

11

the desk, leaving the two garage sale bargain chairs for Claudia and her sister.

"Should I sit down?" Claudia laughed a nervous laugh and gripped the back of the chair.

"I think you should."

A million things ran through her head as she came around in front of the chair and took a seat. Was something wrong with Justin? No, that wouldn't have been a subject for a girl meeting. Girl meetings were for things where everyone needed the strength of the others to get through it. But her mind drew a blank as to what else it could be.

Zoe grabbed her hand, and Claudia shot her sister a grateful look. Whatever it was, they could get through it together, just like everything else.

May tapped her fingers together under her nose, scooted back and forth on the chair, and cleared her throat.

"Come on. I can take it, whatever it is. You can tell me." Claudia braced herself for the news. It had been bad enough when May's father had a heart attack a month ago, requiring the most recent girl meeting. Claudia and her former father-in-law, Roger Drake, hadn't ever been close, but it was still sad to see her son's grandfather in the hospital.

"I just wanted to warn you..."

Claudia leaned forward in her chair, taking her sister with her. "Yes?"

"Well, I just wanted to warn you that..."

"I'm not going to survive this if you only say one new word every time."

May made eye contact with Zoe, who tightened her grip on Claudia's hand. "I just wanted to warn you that

Brad and I are going to have a visitor for the next week or so."

"Ooo-kaayy." Claudia drew out the word, feeling her stomach sink. No visitor of May's would ever be a problem for her except one. And that one person was the only one who would necessitate an emergency girl meeting.

"Peter is on his way home." May's words tumbled out over each other.

Yep, that was the one.

"What the hell?" Zoe took the words right out of her mouth again.

"Yeah, what in the world is that all about?" Claudia gripped Zoe's hand until her sister winced. "Sorry," she said, letting her go, trying to settle back into hard plastic.

"No, that's all right. It's a shock to me, too."

"Explain, May. Why didn't we know about this earlier?" Claudia tried to get comfortable in the chair and failed miserably.

May dropped her head into her hands and shook her hair. Her speech was muffled by her hands when she said, "Dad called him after the heart attack, and Peter is coming to help with the house. I didn't know exactly when he was coming, and I didn't want to alarm you, in case he backed out." She tried a smile, but it failed, as far as Claudia was concerned. "Also, I thought if I gave you less time, you wouldn't have a chance to make excuses to not come to my house when I invite you this Sunday."

Claudia rocked back. She couldn't process it all. "Your *father* called Peter to come help with the house? Your father—the man who wouldn't even tell Peter that his son was born, because it was finals week—is going to pull him away from his precious work to help with the house you already run by yourself? And Peter's coming back to town?" Life just didn't get any worse than this. The bad chair at her back didn't help the bad news, either.

"Yes, to both, and you'll see Peter Sunday at the lunch for my dad."

"No, I won't." Apparently it could.

"Please." May broke out the sad eyes, but Claudia was determined to ignore them.

"I really do not want to be in the same room with...Peter...if I don't have to." She'd almost said "the bastard," but that wouldn't help things, as this bastard was May's brother. It was no secret how Claudia felt about the man who'd walked out on her before their son was born. Sure, for the most part it had all worked out for the best. Life with Peter would have been worse than what she'd managed on her own. But that didn't mean she wanted to have contact with the man who hadn't even bothered to send his kid a card since his third birthday.

"You have to go," May said, finally lifting her head from her hand and piercing Claudia with a look. "I've known you for a lot of years, but you don't owe my father or my family anything, Claude, I get that. But I'm going to have to pull the friendship card and ask you to please be there." The puppy-dog eyes were used shamelessly. "You can even bring Zoe. My dad has some weird notion that he has to distribute his worldly possessions now, while he's still alive, to see them go to the right person."

"You're damn right she's bringing me."

14

A headache roared behind Claudia's eyes, compounded by the metal digging into her elbow and the plastic trying to work its way under her shoulder blades. She couldn't think for all the emotions, memories, and anger running through her. But beneath all of that, a part of her wanted to see what May's dad had to say. And Peter no longer had any effect on her. It had been over ten years since he'd walked out on her at three months pregnant, seven years since she'd heard from him at all. His power to hurt had long since faded. She was sure of it. It hadn't been tested until now, since he'd always stayed far away, but she could stand being in the same room with him for an hour or so without puncturing his head with her high heel.

"Fine," she said, raising a hand to stop the bickering going on between Zoe and May. It wasn't worth fighting over. He wasn't worth fighting over. And if she didn't like what Roger Drake felt her son needed, there was nothing that said she had to keep it.

"Fine?" Zoe and May said at the same time.

"Yes, fine. I'll go. Peter has nothing on me anymore. In fact it will be interesting to see him after all this time. It's not like I haven't thought of him in one way or the other over the years." Like when she had used one of his yearbook pictures as a dart board. "We did share something, but he can't hurt me at this point."

"Wow," Zoe said. "You're a lot bigger person than I am. But we need to do some serious shopping, if you're going to see an old flame. He needs to know what he missed out on."

He missed out on his son's whole life, Claudia thought, but she wasn't going to bring that up. In fact, she wouldn't bring up Justin at all, other than to say thanks or no thanks at the meeting. She didn't even have to make contact with Peter during the lunch if she didn't want to. But she would look astounding, in case he decided to look at her. Nothing better than having a chance to make an ex-boyfriend regret that ex part.

"All right." She put her hands on her knees and rose from the uncomfortable chair. "Anyone have any appointments this afternoon?"

When the two other women shook their heads, she said, "Then shopping it is. And while we're out, we really need to get some new chairs for this office. These are ridiculous. We need to be happy, rich owners, not stiff ones." And she needed to have her head checked, if that was what she'd decided to cling to so she didn't have to think about sitting in the same room with Peter again.

****

"I'm worn through." Claudia threw her bags onto the side table in the entryway of her apartment over their shop, then threw herself on the couch. She could happily sleep, or at least rest, for the next ten to fifteen days.

"Me, too." Zoe lowered her bags to the floor and stretched her back. "Power shopping is not my idea of a good time. I much prefer being able to look at the stuff in a leisurely manner instead of feeling so rushed. I like to shop, but not like we're on some sort of recon mission. Jeez." Zoe took the big chair in the corner and rested her head against the low, rounded back.

"May had to go home and deal with some family stuff. We needed to get done as soon as possible." And Claudia couldn't be happier. Her feet were killing her, and her stomach churned with all the things she hadn't let herself think about since May's announcement. Three more calls from Nate, and now she wasn't sure she wanted to answer him at all. He was not going to be pleased that Peter was back in town.

"I hate to leave you alone right now, but I really have to get back to Decadence to see if I have any other orders to fill." Zoe said but made no move to get out of the chair.

"Eh, don't worry about it. I'm just going to hang out here for the next twenty minutes, until Justin gets home from school, and then I'm taking him to Mom's."

"And then you have the pony date. Excuse me, the stale cookie date. Have fun with that."

Claudia frowned at her sister.

"You know I'm right, but you're so stubborn you're going to have to see it yourself. I get it." Zoe rose from the chair and whisked her pale blonde hair over her shoulder. "At least you can put Justin to bed when you get home from said date and kick back, since it's a school night. Maybe he won't give you any lip for at least one night."

Claudia spent a moment wishing she looked as fresh and young as Zoe. Three years separated them, but sometimes Claudia felt it was more like twenty.

"Justin has a lot going on lately." She pressed her fingers to her temples. "This whole new morbid pre-will thing from Roger certainly isn't going to help with that."

"Not unless he gets something really cool. Then I bet he'll be fine."

"But what about Peter being in town?" Her stomach churned again. "Do you think I should ask him to see Justin while he's here?" That was the big question that had been gnawing at her for the past few hours. Would Justin be devastated if he knew his father had been here but hadn't bothered to see him?

"Absolutely not. I don't think you should let that scum near you or Justin beyond the lunch you're determined to go to. He gave up that privilege a long time ago when he left without a backwards glance." Zoe stomped to emphasize her point and Claudia was reminded again how young she was. Twenty-five and still relatively ignorant of the way things worked. Though she had the operation of the flower shop down to a science, she hadn't been tested much in matters of the heart.

"I'm not sure what I'm going to do. But I do know we need to at least be civil to Peter at that lunch or you're not going to be in the room for too long. I don't want to antagonize him. I don't even want to look at him. So don't call attention to me by being a brat."

Zoe's answer to that was sticking her tongue out as she took the back stairs down to Decadence. Nice. Sunday ought to be a freaking blast.

And now she had to go get ready for her date with Edward-of-the-possible-toupee. What had happened to her excitement about the eight-thousand-dollar check and feeling as if her life was finally on the right track?

Chapter Two

Nate West grabbed the ringing phone as he stepped out of the shower. Slinging a towel around his hips, he walked into his master bedroom and pressed the talk button.

"Hey, Claudia. What's up? You have another huge check to deposit? Or are you finally returning all the phone calls you've been avoiding from me? I don't get why you have a cell, if you're never going to answer it." He laughed and waited for her to laugh, too. But she didn't, and silence hung in the dead space of the phone wire. "Claudia?"

Throat clearing that sounded like Claudia, but nothing else. Had someone hijacked her phone?

"Claudia?"

"Yeah, I'm here, sorry. I was trying to clear my head from all the Lysol and perfume I just had to use. That boy is going to get his rear end grounded."

This ought to be good. Justin stories always were. He loved that kid, but he did not envy Claudia having to deal with his shenanigans sometimes.

"What did he do now?" He settled back on his bed with his arms crossed behind his head. He didn't have anywhere to be tonight and had some time to kill before he made himself dinner. Telling her about Peter could wait a minute.

"Well, how about we stick with this afternoon

only, since I don't have time for the whole day. Let's just say I smelled something foul when I walked past his bedroom. I went in armed with Lysol and came out with a peanut butter and jelly sandwich that looked like it had petrified under the bed, except it smelled horrendous. I sprayed and sprayed and sprayed. Then hit myself with an extra dose of perfume just to clear my nose. I probably reek like a whorehouse, but whatever."

"That's disgusting." But he was laughing.

"You're telling me. And don't you dare laugh about it in front of him. I don't want to encourage him."

"You know I'd never do that. Whenever I'm around him I try to be on my best behavior."

She sighed, and it sounded weary. He didn't like Claudia to sound weary. "Do you want me to come pick him up for a little? I could take him to the batting cages or out for dinner. Maybe the skate park? I have the night free. You could come, too."

She sniffed. He hoped to God she wasn't crying.

"Would you mind?" she asked, her voice stronger. "My mother just called to cancel on taking Justin for the night, and I have a date."

"Edward?" He did not particularly like the guy the one time he'd met him, but he and Claudia had always stayed out of each other's love lives. He wasn't going to interfere now if she wanted to be with some egghead.

"Yes, Edward. He's going to be here in an hour and a half. Can I drop Justin off now, or is that too quick?"

"Bring him now. We'll grill and then play some games. We'll be fine, and I'll have a little talk with him about cleanliness." Of course, he should probably clean his house first, before trying to give advice on the topic.

She laughed, and that sounded much more like the Claudia he'd known since they were little. "Yeah, you do that. Let me know how it works out. And thanks for stepping in at the last minute, Nate. I really appreciate it."

"It's always my pleasure. It is not my pleasure to tell you something else, though."

"I've had about enough with cryptic today. What else do you have to add to my plate? I'm on my third helping as it is."

There was that weariness again. It pulled at something in his chest. But he had to tell her. "I saw Peter today in town."

"Yeah, I heard. May told me he'll be here for a few weeks helping with their dad's house. Thanks for letting me know, though, so I wouldn't be taken off guard. I'll get through this, Nate, like I always do."

Weariness sounded almost like defeat. That was not like Claudia. She was a fighter, scrappy to the last. "You know I'm here if you need someone."

"I know. You've always been there for me. It's only a few weeks. I'll survive. But first I have to go on this date, and I really appreciate you helping at the last minute. I'll see you in a few."

She hung up and so did he, putting his phone on the dresser before pulling out a T-shirt and some jeans that had probably seen better days.

He put the towel around his neck and made a quick trip to the backyard to crank up the gas grill. This would be much better than what he had been planning, which was nothing.

Five minutes later, the front door flew open and

Justin came running into the kitchen. "Nate, Nate, Nate!"

"Hey, bud, go put your stuff in the living room. Then go see if the grill is hot, like I taught you before. We're going to have burgers and dogs."

"Awesome!" And the kid was off like a shot.

Claudia wandered into the kitchen a second later. "Thanks, Nate. He's really excited to be here."

"It's fine. I like having the guy around. Plus, he'll save me if my brother calls to invite me out for a beer. So I have my own agenda here, too." He laughed. "Seriously, it was a long day putting a new coat of paint on Mrs. Finkey's window frames. Then I had to agree to talk to her grandson about maybe apprenticing with me this summer. It was a headache all the way around, even if he is a good kid. But now I just want to hang out, you know?"

"Yeah," she said, but she was looking at his cabinets and cleared her throat again.

"Anything wrong?"

"Nope. Nothing new since we talked five minutes ago." She gave him a big smile, but he wasn't convinced.

"You're sure? Do you want to talk about the Peter thing?"

"Absolutely sure, and 'no' on the Peter thing. Little ears and all that. It'll be fine. I should get going, though. I have to finish getting ready for my date, and I don't want to be late."

"Okay, have fun with Edward. And don't think about the other."

"Will do," she said, before giving him a mock salute and heading back toward the front of the house.

He hummed as he took some of his mom's homemade potato salad out of the refrigerator. He didn't think Claudia would really have any fun with that Edward guy, but he wasn't going to be the one to tell her she was wasting her time. She needed someone who wanted her to be herself. Someone she could wear heels with, instead of those ugly flats she'd just been sporting. He didn't let himself think about her as a real woman often because he didn't want to mess with their friendship, but she looked damn fine in a pair of heels. As for Peter, if she wasn't overly concerned, then he guessed he wasn't either. He'd be there to protect her, as he always had, but with Claudia sometimes you had to let her fight her own battles.

Justin whooped from the backyard. Time to play with his favorite guy and forget about Claudia and her date. She was a big girl and had known her mind for a whole lot more years than he had. He just hoped there was something worthy in Edward that he couldn't see but that worked for Claudia.

****

Claudia spritzed the back of her knees with her atomizer and, to allow the scent to air out, walked around in the black flats that went horribly with her flirty, asymmetrical skirt. She hated flats, but after their third date, she'd caved and bought the terrible shoes for the first time in her life. Edward was an inch shorter than Claudia, and she didn't want to tower over him.

She would never tower over Nate.

The doorbell rang, slicing neatly through her thoughts. A glance at her watch told her it was Edward. He was exactly three minutes early, as he always was. And she had become just as predictable. Add that to her list of things that had gone wrong in the past ten years. That damn list seemed to grow every day.

Walking on the hardwood floor through the apartment on her way to the front door, there was no satisfying clacking of pencil-thin heels to remind Claudia she was a woman going on a hot date. Instead she felt twelve years old, listening to the muffled shuffle of her horrible flats.

Claudia pulled the heavy oak door of her upstairs apartment open and stared at Edward. The regular script would begin in a moment.

He didn't disappoint.

Step One. "Hello, Claudia. My, you look lovely this evening."

Step Two. Edward checked his watch and tapped a finger to the glass face. "Well, we should be going if we want to make the play." This was the only part that ever changed, the location of their date. Even his voice never altered from the singsong cadence. For all she cared he could be selling the hottest thing in vacuum cleaners.

And *Step Three*. A perfunctory kiss on the cheek delivered far enough away from her lips so as not to be the least bit tantalizing. Then they were out the door.

With her hand resting lightly on Edward's elbow, Claudia was escorted down the wooden steps of the outside staircase and led to the dull brown four-door sedan. She had nothing against sedans, she drove one herself, but this car was so blah. The interior was also brown, and Claudia felt as if she were being swallowed by a huge puddle of suffocating mud. Suffocating was a good word when applied to Edward, but she'd successfully ignored giving in to that thought for three months. She wasn't going to succumb now. Especially since it was all Zoe's fault that she was finding flaws in Edward. Flaws she hadn't had a problem with before. Damn Zoe's cake speech and the way Nate had taken her off guard with his body to die for when she'd just wanted to anonymously fantasize.

Edward started the car with a methodical movement of his hand, and they were off. She tried to break the rhythm of the night by talking right away instead of waiting for him to make the first conversational move as he liked, just to see if she could shake things up a bit. He wasn't a bad person or a mean man, but damn it, she wanted fireworks and spontaneity. Cake instead of three-day-old cookies.

She wished she'd never heard of cake. It was plaguing her now.

She tried to settle into the familiar rhythm of their once-weekly date and found herself just a half beat off.

Thirty minutes later, over lobster bisque and wine, Claudia concluded Zoe was right, though she'd never tell her and inflate her ego. Although she was reasonably sure Edward did not in fact wear a toupee, she was thinking he might have had hair plugs put in. How had she not realized that in the three months they had been dating? If she were honest with herself, Claudia would admit she probably had noticed but just shut it up tight with every other misgiving she'd ever experienced over dating the man. She had reasons for wanting this relationship to continue along the comfortable rut they'd worn in the road. Edward was stable and dependable.

And boring, a little voice whispered.

The smile on her face faltered. Claudia put it right

back on and bumped up the wattage. Edward was looking at her expectantly, and she was horrible for having these unkind thoughts about him.

So what if he had hair plugs, or didn't live a highly passionate and volatile life? That was precisely why she'd gone out with him the first time and the second time. After that it just felt like a routine. One she didn't have the energy to break.

Plus, he had impeccable table manners, which were hard to come by these days.

"So," Edward said, with a huge smile that made Claudia a little bit nervous. "How was your day?"

She was absurdly pleased he asked, because she had great—better than great, awesome—news. This was why she didn't pay attention to the hair plugs—if there were any. "Well, I made a really good sale today and lined up three other jobs. I'm really excited about..."

"Good, good," he interrupted. "I'm glad to hear you're making some money at your little business." He laughed, and it sounded like a braying donkey or even, possibly, a huge jackass of a pony.

The smile was still frozen on her face, but Claudia was beginning to feel her temper boil at the base of her spine. He had deliberately placed emphasis on "some" and "little," and it made her grind her molars. Her right hand dropped to her lap to clench the white linen napkin in a grip like a wrestler's. The urge swelled to yank some of those plugs out.

But Edward missed every telltale sign because he was still talking. "And I suppose when we are married, perhaps—and I stress *perhaps*—you can keep it as a *side* business. But you will have access to my money, and I will expect you to concentrate on entertaining instead of being a *baker*. Your skills would be better suited to our home."

Okay, more emphasized words, and they were all bad. Who was this, and what had happened to Edward? The Edward Claudia knew was mild-mannered, even malleable to some extent. At least that was the way she'd always viewed him. He'd never been demanding and snobby. Or had he? Little pieces of previous evenings spent together flitted through Claudia's mind. As they started piling up, one on top of another, it occurred to her she'd never paid enough attention to really know him. Well, this was not going to be the happy celebration she had expected.

"Edward," she said, trying to discreetly get his attention during his monologue. "Edward," she tried again, a little louder. Then realizing she wasn't getting through to him, she banged her fork on the side of his fine china dish of sautéed scallops and finally managed to break his chain of ridiculous words. As well as silence the entire restaurant, but she was too angry to notice.

"Yes, dear?" he said, as if he hadn't heard her at all prior to the fork banging. That was certainly disturbing.

"Edward, I don't think our relationship is going in the direction you're talking about." Might as well be blunt when you're laying it on the line. "I have no intention of being a hostess for your stockbroker buddies and their wives, and I have no intention of Decadence being a sideline business. It's my career and I love what I do." Clinking glasses, silverware and conversations resumed as the muted volume of Claudia's voice caused everyone to wrongly assume the fork banging was a momentary distraction.

"Well, of course you do. But when we get married, there will be no need for you to work for the masses in your little shop. You could, of course, continue to make some cakes on special order, and for our dinners, but I don't want a wife of mine working for a living when it's not necessary."

If there was one thing Claudia could not stand, it was men who patted you on the head and dismissed everything you said because it was not as important as what they thought or said themselves. The fabled temper inched closer to her throat, where she knew it would spew from her mouth in a long string of frightening words and a scene that might just make the front page of Tea Time, Teasdale's one and only daily paper. Inhaling deeply, she caught the scent of seafood and candle wax as she tried to calm herself.

But she failed because he'd started talking over her again, and that she wouldn't tolerate. "Excuse me, *Eddie*." She used some emphasis of her own and put as much attitude in her voice as she could muster. That shut him up and had his beady eyes bulging from behind his wire-rim glasses. What had she ever seen in this guy? Why had her mother ever introduced them?

"Let's get a few things straight," she said, and stood abruptly. Silence descended in the restaurant for the second time in two minutes. "I would never marry you, you pompous ass, if you had ever bothered to ask instead of just wrongly assuming. I do not have my shop as some kind of hobby until some schmuck like you comes along and whisks me away in your boring, brown, four-door sedan. And last but by no means least, you need to get hair plugs that actually cover all of your bald spot. No one has an inch strip of baldness above their ears."

She threw her napkin on the table and stalked away from the idiot she'd wasted the last three months of her life on. The shush of her flats on the polished wood floors echoed in the stillness of the upscale establishment.

She was throwing away these damn shoes as soon as she got home.

She was done with the guy who thought she was some kind of useful decoration, like a chair you set up next to the door to hold your coat. The next time she saw her mother, she was going to ask her what on earth she'd been thinking when she set Claudia up with this idiot. In the meantime, Claudia had to ask herself why she had stayed so long with someone who did nothing for her.

Exiting the restaurant, she pointed herself toward home. Dammit, Zoe had been right about more than just the bad hair. He was a jerk and not worth her time. Where was her cake? A part of her wanted to find out what it was like to be with a man who wanted her for her. She hadn't been with anyone like that in years, since high school and Justin's father, Peter, if she were honest. And apparently she was being honest right now.

She was honest enough to admit she wanted cake with all the icing. Honest enough to listen to her sweet tooth singing.

Walking the few short blocks home, she pulled her wrap a little tighter around her shoulders. It might be April on the calendar, but the air was cooler than normal, especially after the above-average heat of the day. At least she'd been able to make her dramatic exit without tripping over anything or needing to figure out how to get home. Teasdale had its drawbacks, but you couldn't fault a town where you could pretty much walk from any point to your house. It certainly suited her just fine this evening.

And she still had several hours stretched out in front of her. Justin would be disappointed if she picked him up from Nate's too early. She'd had brief thoughts of ending up in bed with Edward this evening, since that's where things were probably heading after the amount of time they'd spent together. But now she was glad she didn't have to expend the energy for so little payoff. Ha! Talk about three-day-old cookies! With Edward it was probably better done in the dark, with the covers up, and when she was half-asleep. She'd have bet her best whisk that there was almost no reason for her to be there except as a substitute for a hole in the mattress.

But she wasn't going to go there right now, since she wouldn't have to deal with it ever again. Well, something good had come of this whole mess then, hadn't it?

A brisk wind picked up as she rounded the last corner on her way home. Discreet security lights glowed from behind the large windows fronting Decadence. One of her mom's original wedding dress designs stood in the near window, a wonder of lace and satin and white tulle draped over a high-backed chair as if patiently waiting for the bride to come in with her entourage and get ready for her special day. The dress was timeless and had lain there for the last twenty years.

Her mother had started this shop with just her

dresses when Claudia was eight. Memories flitted through her mind of dancing in and out between the racks of dresses, the bright jewel tones and pure whites, the soft satiny fabric and rougher tulle brushing against her shoulders. Of standing in the back of the dressing room watching all the pretty ladies try on their party dresses or wedding dresses.

Her favorites, though, were the girls who came in to get their prom dresses or formals for parties and dances. She would chat them up, learn all about their favorite boys and how they were going to do their hair. She'd thought at first she would follow in her mom's footsteps and make dresses. But when people had started talking about the food and the cakes and the pastries that were going to be served, she found her true calling at twelve when she made her first Barbie cake.

And she'd fed it to Nate West, who ate it even though she'd used brown sugar instead of regular sugar and baking powder instead of baking soda. But he'd eaten the first piece and another, icing smeared on his lips and little jimmy sprinkles falling from his fingers.

She hadn't thought of that in years. Standing in front of the middle display window, she caught her reflection in the backlit glass superimposed over the five-tier wedding cake. A winding trellis of glossy ivy wrapped along the layers, interspersed with velvety purple pansies and glistening yellow irises made of confectioners' sugar.

A parade of images flashed through her mind. Making cakes, laughing, flour on her face, every step taken toward doing what she loved. The setback and the joy of having Justin at eighteen, throwing off her plans to attend culinary school but bringing such happiness into her life with his smiles and gurgling, his first steps, his first words.

And, through it all, there was Nate. In every memory. In every way. He'd waited with a blue teddy bear and miniature baseball glove while she'd sweated and screamed through labor. He'd held Justin in his big gangly eighteen-year-old hands and whispered something into her son's ear that she'd never been able to figure out or get Nate to tell her.

She took two steps to stand in front of Zoe's display window with its baskets and bouquets, beautiful dried arrangements of blossoms that promised hope and love of many different kinds. Reaching out a hand, she stopped an inch from touching the glass and ghosted her finger over the white-and-red rose bridal spray. One day, long ago, she had wanted to get married, and then her dreams had changed.

Well, she could change them again, couldn't she? Why, just because things didn't originally work out the way she'd planned, did she think she couldn't have it all? Just on a different timetable and maybe with some small changes.

Standing back from the display windows, she took in all three at the same time and saw the harmony in their love and labor. It was Peter at the beginning, the boy she'd thought would be a man when he found out they were going to have a baby. But it was Nate who brought her ice chips, Nate who paced the halls, Nate who picked Justin up when he fell, Nate who held her when she couldn't believe she had a five-year-old in kindergarten at twenty-three, Nate who'd poured wine down her, laughed with her over pictures…

And Nate who would be with her until the end with

Justin. She didn't need cake. She had the best of both worlds with Nate as a father figure without the messiness of a real and intimate relationship.

Perhaps she should just concentrate on getting through these next few weeks, with her ex in town and several weddings that needed cakes, and then see where she was at the end. Adding a cake craving on top of that was only going to make things messier. And she needed messy right now like she needed a fly in her best butter cream icing.

First things first, though: she was going to tell her mother to stop matchmaking. She was tired of the string of guys who made her feel about as feminine as a roll of toilet paper.

Stalking up the outside stairs to her home, she huffed out her frustration. She'd stopped thinking of herself as a woman after Peter, the father of her child, had walked away and gone on his merry way to college. Part of her had been so relieved he'd finally left, taking his childish temper tantrums and complete lack of help with him. The other part hadn't been able to believe she was going to be the sole responsible person for a baby who would be born in six months. Thank God Nate had been there to help.

She shoved the door of her apartment open and stormed through. No, she wouldn't think about that for another second, as a matter of fact. She at least wanted cake in her life, and putting it off until some other time was not going to give her sweet tooth any satisfaction.

She needed her son to be happy and healthy, her shop to thrive, and a roof over her head. And maybe, just maybe, she'd see about Nate, if the timing was right. Maybe.

All conditions met, except for the happy son part, but that she could work on with him. Nate often helped to make him happy and teach him about life, too. She would be lost without him. It would be work to fit everything in, but she wasn't afraid of a little hard work. She'd been at it for almost eleven years at this point.

She shared her apartment with her sister, but she owned it. She shared her business with two of the best women in the world, and her son would eventually get over himself, even if she had to force him.

Her love life was her own. Or at least it would be, once she got her hands on one very delicious piece of rear end labeled Nate West.

Of course her resolve didn't last much past getting into her room. Who was she kidding? The problems with going after Nate were already stacking up in her head.

"Ugh!" After kicking off her shoes, Claudia threw herself on her bed and dropped her hand over her eyes.

"I told you I was right," Zoe said, startling Claudia.

Where had she come from? And she hadn't even tried to keep the smugness out of her voice.

"You're my sister. Aren't you supposed to hold the 'I told you so' line and just commiserate with me?"

"Probably, but not this time. He isn't right for you."

"Yeah, I figured that out for myself tonight, thanks very much."

"No charge." Zoe flopped down on the bed next to Claudia, stuck her legs up in the air, and seemed to be contemplating the meaning of her toes.

"You were wrong about the rug, though. It was hair

plugs. Poorly done hair plugs." Claudia couldn't believe she had dismissed that. She certainly hadn't missed it, but she'd ignored it all along.

"I was still in the ball park, though. You should always listen to your little sister when it comes to these kinds of things."

Claudia smacked her in the face with a pillow. "At least I'm out there still trying to date and be semi-normal."

Zoe grabbed the pillow and tucked it behind her head. "Yeah, well, you'll never really be normal, semi or otherwise. I applaud you for sticking your neck and body out there trying to find Mr. Right."

"I hear a 'but' in there."

"Absolutely. Isn't there always a 'but' in there?" Claudia didn't make contact with the pillow this time. Zoe snatched it out of her hands and tucked it behind her head, too. "But you need to stop listening to Mom, who obviously needs her eyes and brain checked if she thought Eddie was right for you."

"At least I'm actually dating."

"I'm actually dating, too, goofus, just not with any intent. I'm only twenty-five, and in no huge hurry to run out and find the Right one, or even the Right For Now one. I'll take the Hung one."

This time Claudia was faster, but she also ended up with her head flat on the comforter while Zoe was propped up like a queen against the headboard with all the pillows. "You're incorrigible."

"And you still have several hours before you have to pick up your precious boy. Maybe you should go to a bar and see what kind of men are hanging out on this fine night. I'll go with you."

"Not going to happen," Claudia said, with her mouth if not her heart. She could see herself out on a club dance floor, maybe shaking what her mama gave her in the arms of a cute guy for the night. While in her mind that might be a pretty picture, she knew it would never happen. But, oh, just the thought… Her hormones were not helping her stay sane.

If only the cute guy would be Nate. Thoughts of what exactly that would entail made her blood pressure spike a few degrees. She fanned herself and blew out a breath.

"Who are you thinking about now, hussy?" Zoe wasn't stupid enough to give up her pillows, so she tapped Claudia on the head with her balled fist. "Jensen Ackles, again?"

"Ha! No, not someone so unattainable." And now she'd just opened a can of worms, because Zoe would eventually find out who was more attainable. And then discuss in detail how Claudia could go about attaining him.

Her sister didn't disappoint. "Who? Who? Who!"

"You sound like an owl."

"You are not going to distract me."

Claudia propped herself up on an elbow, facing Zoe. "I wasn't thinking of anyone in particular."

"Liar." Zoe also turned and propped her hand under her head. "Please tell me you've finally decided to bag the very yummy Nate."

Um. "What?"

"The very yummy Nate. Tell me you've finally decided to look beyond the whole 'he's my best friend' thing and finally jump him like he's never been jumped before."

Now what could she say to that? She had hoped to secretly seduce him and have a kind of friends-with-benefits relationship. Just the cake, please. Would she be able to do that with Zoe hawking over her shoulder?

Definitive answer: No.

"Hmmm," Claudia said to give herself a moment. "No, I wasn't thinking of Nate. I was thinking of Hank, down at the soda shop."

"I'm not that gullible." Zoe smirked. "Hank hasn't moved from his stool with his newspaper and his root beer float since 1985. And he was old then." She tapped her lips with one painted fingernail. "No, I think you definitely get that heat-flash look in your eyes when it comes to Nate."

"A lot you know." Maybe she could get Zoe to play devil's advocate to her lustful thoughts without giving herself away. "Think what it would do to our friendship and to Justin's buddy nights."

"You mean enhance them?"

"No, ruin them if something happened."

"Ah, ha! So you have thought about it." Zoe's lips quirked up in another smug smile.

Claudia grabbed a pillow from under her elbow and threatened her with it. "I have not." Not more than twenty times today, anyway.

"I think you have, and it's coming to the front now, after twenty years, because he's working on the shop and you have to stare at him with his tool belt on every day."

Claudia sputtered. "I have not stared at him in his short-sleeved white T-shirt and thought about his biceps. Looked at his jeans and wanted to be in them. Or glanced at his supple brown leather tool belt with its wrenches and drills and been turned on like a light switch. I'm not going there."

Zoe collapsed back into her pillows, clutching her stomach while she laughed loud and long. "You have to go there and pick up Justin. And, dear sister, since that's not at all what I said, I think you are also on the verge of protesting too much. So I'll leave you to go pick up your son at the guy's house who you don't think of his yummy biceps or his tools. Have fun. Do everything I would."

Zoe jumped off the bed and ran from the bedroom before Claudia could say anything else.

Great. Now she'd have to go face Nate knowing her lust wasn't as carefully hidden as she'd thought it was.

Chapter Three

Nate West groaned on the floor, attacked and quite possibly maimed by the figure looming over him. He'd just been stabbed in the heart with a spatula and was down for the count. "No, Master Zofo, do not deal the death blow, please, I beg of you."

"Bwahahahaha! I can do no less. You have committed treason, and for that you must pay!"

Raising his hand in the air, Nate cowered away from the ten-year-old boy with the apron hanging around his neck and down his back, an old Scooby Doo tie wrapped around his waist to hold his weapons. The boy stood spread-legged, brandishing the deadly spatula.

"There will be no mercy." Justin Bradley, aka Master Zofo—Claudia had always been a big Led Zeppelin fan—jabbed out with the spatula, and Nate thanked God it was made of rubber.

"Hey man, watch the goods."

Justin broke character and started giggling. "Sorry, Nate, I didn't mean to get you in the gonads."

Another giggle. Nate took the opportunity to wrestle the boy to the floor and start his very own torture.

"No, no, no," Justin screamed, laughing the whole time. "Not the Tickle Maruchan."

"Yes, I know I cannot kill the all-powerful,

immortal Master Zofo, but I may vanquish him with tickle."

The doorbell rang, breaking Nate's concentration. It cost him. He tried to crawl to the door, but Justin held onto the back of his thigh and gave a war whoop as they inched their way to the front door. When fingers dug into his ribs, Nate yelled, "Help!" still laughing.

Then Claudia walked in, bent down, and tickled him, too.

"That's not what I meant," he gasped as her fingers assaulted his ribs. He almost got an eyeful of boob when he tried to sit up. But she backed off with a half smile and a flip of her blonde hair.

He cleared his throat and shuffled Justin off his body. "You're no help."

"I wasn't trying to be." The smile stayed in place, kinking up the side of her mouth. "You're a big strong man. I thought you could take it."

Pulling Justin up by his apron strings, Nate set him on his feet and brushed him off, using the time to let his pant legs fall back down from his knees. He tried to figure out what had made that smile different from the ones she normally wore. He was used to her playfulness. How couldn't he be, after almost twenty years in each other's pockets? But there was something vaguely unsettling about that tiny crinkle on the left side.

"Before you ask how the date was, don't." Claudia held up a hand, and her bracelets clinked as they slid down her arm.

He got Justin on his way to the kitchen with a swat to his rear end and told him to get his stuff together. "That bad, huh?"

"Didn't I just tell you not to ask?" She crossed her arms over her chest, cocked a hip out to rest against the doorway to the living room, and flipped her hair back over her shoulder, again.

"Sorry, I just thought you'd want to talk about it." Like you always do, he thought but didn't say.

Part of him felt sorry for her. She'd invested a lot of time into that relationship. But the other, bigger, part of him was glad she'd finally realized what an ass the man was. Edward had never been good enough for her, just like all the other men who had come and gone from her life.

"At least that's over," she said, breaking into his thoughts. And then she started blinking really fast and dipped her head down.

"So no more Edward, at all?"

More fluttering eyelashes. Was she having a problem?

"Nope. Edward has gone the way of the cream-filled doughnuts I tried to make in twelfth grade." Crossing her ankles, she bumped the hip out some more and shrugged her shoulder.

"Well, I'm sorry to hear it."

"No, you're not." She tapped him lightly on the arm and stuck her tongue out at him. "You hated him just as much as Zoe did. Don't try to pretend differently."

Thankfully, he was saved by Justin running back into the living room with his arms full of all his stuff. His plastic sword stuck up from his back above his ear, his comic books were crushed against his thin, young chest.

"Ready, Mom. Let's go, let's go!" As Justin ran

back and forth right next to Claudia's non-leaning hip, he nearly knocked her over.

"In a minute," she said, batting her eyelashes again.

Finally, Nate had to ask. "Can I get you something for that?"

The batting stopped, and her gray eyes opened wide. "For what?"

"Well, I think it's stopped. It looked like you had something stuck in your eye there for a minute. I didn't know if you needed to wash it out."

She heaved a sigh, and her eyes went back to normal. "No. No, nothing in my eye, but thanks for the offer." Her shoulders drooped, then she seemed to shake off whatever it was and stood straighter. "Hey, thanks again for watching him on such short notice. It may be a while before I go out on any dates again, so I won't impose on your time."

He ruffled Justin's hair. "You know it's no hardship to watch my guy. It doesn't only have to be when you need to go out, does it?"

"Um, no, of course not." She uncrossed her arms. He'd never seen her so stiff before.

"Are you sure something's not wrong? You look uncomfortable." He laughed to release some of the weird tension in the air. "Or is it just the new shoes?" He hadn't seen her wear heels on a date in months.

"Yeah, you know how I hate wearing flats, and now I don't have to anymore. I'm going to symbolically burn those when I get home. You like the new ones?" She turned her ankle to showcase the almost-three-inch heel, and he made the appropriate noises.

She returned to Justin and crouched down to his level. "Ready to go, buddy?"

"Yep. I was ready to go like twenty minutes ago."

"It wasn't twenty minutes." Nate eyed him from beneath lowered eyebrows. "Your mom just got here, and you know it. No games."

"All right, all right. Yeesh! You sure are bossy."

"And you're short, but I don't hold that against you," Nate shot back, ruffling Justin's hair.

"So on that note," Claudia said, giving the back of Justin's head a flick, "we need to go. Thanks again, Nate. We'll see you soon." That kicky little smile hitched up the corner of her mouth when she looked back over her shoulder as they were leaving.

He shut the front door, not knowing what the hell was going on with Claudia. Maybe she was developing some kind of facial tick. That would be sad.

****

Justin was in bed finally and settled down for the night when Claudia came back into the living room and accepted a glass of wine from Zoe. The horrendous shoes had literally been burned and thrown into the dumpster out back. But even that hadn't made her feel better.

"I was a mess."

Zoe sat back in the loveseat covered in throw pillows and two afghans, her legs tucked under her, looking relaxed, while Claudia felt twisted into the remnants of a used icing bag.

"I highly doubt that," Zoe said and took a sip of her own wine. She sagged back against the sofa and blew out a breath. "There's no way you are that out of practice. You used to have a wicked flirt going on."

"Yeah, almost eleven years ago. That's not exactly a recommendation."

Zoe waved a hand in the air. "You don't need a recommendation. It's like riding a bike."

"I haven't ridden a bike in almost seven years. You're not making me feel any better. I was an abysmal failure with Nate. He asked me if I needed to wash out my eye! He probably thinks I have some kind of new disease or something." The horror of it was she did feel like she was contracting some kind of flu bug. Or maybe it was just her complete ineptness at catching the eye of a man who wasn't three inches shorter and balding. Men like that flocked to her and she didn't have to do a damn thing. Yet now when she wanted something more... "I made a complete ass out of myself."

Zoe snickered. "Seriously, I highly doubt he even noticed, if he thought you needed some eyewash."

"You are not helping. Again. Why does this always seem so easy when you do it, but I fail miserably?" And she did mean miserably. How embarrassing. She'd thought she was using some of her best moves, and he'd offered her first aid.

"We'll work on it. As long as you put yourself completely in my hands, I can have you back in excellent flirting condition within days." She arched an eyebrow. "But you have to put yourself completely in my hands." The other eyebrow joined the first. "Completely."

The twisted icing bag burst and splattered. She could already tell this was not going to be her best idea. She'd see how she felt after some much-needed sleep.

****

After getting Justin off to school with minimum fuss the next day, Claudia made her way downstairs.

She was not going let her sister tutor her on flirting. She admitted she might have gotten off to a rocky start with Nate. She'd simply been a bit tongue-tied after seeing him with his shirt partially off—those abs had truly been stumble-worthy. But if she wanted Nate to see her as something more than his best friend of the last two decades, then she'd have to be herself. Not some floozy.

She thought about that as she took cake orders and directed three calls to Zoe for flower orders and another call to May for a dress for an upcoming fiftieth high school reunion at the American Legion down the road.

She had a list a mile long for the upcoming days— six weddings over the next two weeks, and a handful of anniversaries, along with the cakes for that reunion— and now her mother was making noise about retiring. She'd come in this morning all chipper with her announcement, totally missing how rocked Claudia felt about her leaving permanently.

Mona Bradley had been in talks with May about May filling in more and eventually taking over as a partial owner of the shop, but now was not the time to step up the timetable, with the wedding season upon them. Despite wanting to tell their mom to please wait until September or after, Claudia had sent Zoe to talk with their uncle (and lawyer) to see what it would take to allow Mona to retire. Normally, Claudia would have jumped at the chance to see Uncle Al, but her schedule was filled to the limit.

How she thought she was going to fit in a romance—or even some kind of friends-with-benefits arrangement—was beyond her. Quite honestly, she told herself, she had waited this long, she could wait a little bit longer.

The grandfather clock in the corner of the cake shop struck three, and Claudia waited expectantly for Justin to come in after getting off the bus.

Cleaning up the counter over the front display case, Claudia hoped it had been a good day. They had a good streak of days coming, as far as she was concerned, to make up for the crappy ones recently. In fact, she planned on running by him the idea of going to the batting cages after dinner on Friday. Maybe it would keep the good mood rolling.

Her son came hustling through the door as the last gong struck. He was full of chatter and actually hugged her before throwing his bag behind the counter.

Claudia struggled for a moment with what to do. He knew he was supposed to put his backpack into the small office so things were not a mess in the shop, but they were having such a good day, with his mouth going a mile a minute. Did she really want to potentially ruin this little piece of bliss they were experiencing? Ten years of mothering by herself kicked in, though, and she just couldn't let it slide.

"Hey, bud, you need to pick up that bag and put it in the office, okay?" she said with a smile on her face, hoping it would keep the mood light.

A scowl briefly flickered over Justin's face before he picked up the backpack and trudged into the office.

At least there hadn't been a blowup or a meltdown. She would have bet her odds were only 50/50 on either outcome.

He came back out just as Nate, dressed in another pair of low-slung jeans and a tight, white T-shirt, came strolling through the door. The outfit was so like yesterday that all the spit dried up in her mouth. Why had she never realized how very sexy her best friend was? How had he been hiding under her nose this whole time? Was she really that blind? Part of her desperately wanted him to notice her in the same way after all these years. The other part of her knew she was so going to hell for lusting after him—astounding abs or not.

"Hey, Claudia." Nate smiled, and something started to simmer down below. Justin came tearing across the room at that moment, like freezing water on her libido parade.

She still hadn't justified how she could go after Nate when it might put Justin's relationship with him in jeopardy. But those dimples were making it not seem to matter so much.

Justin was again talking a mile a minute, so Claudia couldn't get a word in edgewise. Here was the boy she liked to remember instead of the sullen almost-teenager who had taken over her son's body.

"So, anyway," Justin said, all innocent eyes. "When are you going to take me to the batting cages again?"

Claudia sighed. He knew better than to invite himself to stuff, and hadn't she just thought to take him to the batting cages herself?

She jumped in before Nate could say a word. "Hon, Nate is working on the store and has several other sites going. He probably doesn't have time right now. But I made time Friday night, and I was going to take you myself." He might need the distraction if he had to be in the same room with his absentee sperm donor.

She didn't blame him for the skepticism on his

face. She hadn't been doing much with him lately beyond making dinner and telling him to do his homework. If she were honest with herself, she had to admit it was because he was being a pain in the ass. But that was no excuse, or at least not a good one.

"*You* are going to take me to the batting cages? *You?*" Justin crossed his arms and gave her his face of disbelief. It was not one she liked, quite honestly.

"Hey, guy, I wouldn't look a gift horse in the mouth, Justin." Nate put a hand on her son's shoulder and squeezed. "If your mom says she's going to take you, maybe you should just be thankful and not lippy. You know what I mean?" Nate removed his hand, then stood with his arms crossed at his chest, the muscles of his biceps bulging in a way she had never noticed before.

She did not need the distraction.

"Okay, so with that settled, what's up, Nate?" Maybe he had gotten a clue about her flirting and had come back to get something started. She could go with that distraction. She almost started batting her eyelashes, then stopped herself in time. She did not want any more offers of first aid.

"Yeah," Nate said, looking like he always had. "I promised you dinner to celebrate your sale yesterday, and you demanded I pay. So I'm here to pay up."

"I thought you said this weekend." She leaned on the case instead of batting her eyelashes and wondered if he would notice her cleavage. So much for not acting like a floozy.

He didn't notice at all. "Tonight works for me, too, as long as you don't have any other plans. Like with some new guy your mom set you up with now that

48

Edward is history." He looked adorable with his lopsided grin and hair that should have been trimmed two weeks ago.

"We'd love to go," Justin said inviting himself along. "And, Mom, you didn't tell me Edward was gone. Good riddance, as Aunt Zoe says! We should celebrate that, too!"

Jeez. "Honey, we're going to have to celebrate another night. Aunt Zoe and I have a lot to discuss about the shop. Sorry," she said turning to Nate. "Can I take a rain check? Maybe it would be nice to have dinner next week after this thing Sunday is done. Can we make it for Monday?"

"Absolutely." Nate tucked his hands into his pockets, straining the denim in interesting ways. "Rain check it is."

And then she watched him walk out of Decadence, wondering if she shouldn't have just gone and taken Justin to Zoe and taken Zoe's advice. Damn!

****

Nate drove home from Decadence, not sure what to make of that conversation with Claudia. On the surface he wasn't angry that she had turned him down for dinner. He'd gone in knowing she might have other things to do tonight. However, he was baffled.

He didn't know what was going on with Claudia, but something was. If he had been a better friend, he would have stayed around or insisted she go to dinner with him. They could have talked out whatever was going on. As much as he was a guy and usually oblivious to a lot of what went on around him—his mother's words—he didn't miss the signs that Claudia was in distress.

His first guess was Peter being in town and what a shock that must be. But Claudia was up to anything, as far as he was concerned, and if she said she could handle it, then she could handle it.

But what was with the kinked-up smile? It was vaguely unsettling, and nothing about Claudia had been even mildly unsettling since they were twelve and he realized she was a "girl." He'd suffered a crush but had put it aside when he realized she saw him as a non-guy, her best friend.

Pulling into his driveway, he rested his head back on the seat while the garage door opened. She was strong, and she would get through this, and as always he would be here for her, no matter what. In the meantime, he would keep an eye out for Peter and try to anticipate whatever she might need, from a shoulder to someone running interference.

And hopefully it would be enough. Peter would go home and they could get back to their regular lives. He was comfortable there. Had been for years. If Claudia was going through a tough time now, she would get over it like she always did, and then they would move on. Like they always did.

If Logan's words about following after Claudia like a lovesick puppy followed him into the house, he ignored them. They were unfair and untrue. He always helped out his friend, and he wouldn't stop now.

****

"What do you mean you pissed off our lawyer? How could you make Uncle Al mad? He's one of the easiest-going guys around." Claudia moved from the island in the middle of the kitchen and back to the counter. She slid the cubed chicken into the pan and used her wrist to move some hair off her cheek. She should have gone out to dinner with Nate. Even failing abysmally at flirting would have been better than this new headache.

"Not Uncle Al, he loves me. But for some stupid reason he made me talk with another guy in the same office, and I managed to piss *him* off." Zoe snatched a carrot from the bowl and Claudia smacked her hand with a wooden spoon.

"If you're not going to help with dinner, the least you could do is not eat it before I have a chance to cook it." Standing at the sink, she washed her hands, paying special attention to her nails so she didn't have to turn around just yet. Zoe could be impulsive and defensive. Maybe they should have gone in as a group.

"Why did you piss him off?" She turned around once she had herself under control. "It was a simple enough task. All you had to do was go in and get some information, then come back to let us know what we need to do."

Zoe shrugged and looked down into the depth of the salad bowl as if it had the answers to the universe.

Hmmm.

"He just wasn't very nice to me." Zoe picked a cucumber out of the salad and popped it into her mouth.

Was she trying to avoid making eye contact? Definite hmmm. "What did he do?"

Now, normally Claudia would have her back up and be the first one to defend her sister. She'd already be in the car and on her way down to the law office to smack some sense into this new lawyer guy, Uncle Al or no Uncle Al. But she also knew that Zoe was avoiding meeting her eyes, and Uncle Al was a very good judge of character. Something else was going on.

"He didn't really do anything. But he did rub me the wrong way."

"He rubbed you?" Claudia just wanted to see her reaction.

Sure enough, Zoe's head flew up and her face turned red. "Of course not. I mean, he shook my hand when I left the office. He was fine, okay? Forget I said anything."

"No, I don't think I will forget about it." Honestly, it would give her a chance to think about something other than her failure as a flirt. She'd obsessed all afternoon after talking to Nate and getting turned on by his mere voice. That was not going so well.

So maybe Zoe was having a hard time today too. Then again... "Was he cute?" She leaned back against the counter and crossed her arms over her chest. A smile played over her mouth. She was fully aware it was smug.

Zoe gasped like a carp out of water for a while, and Claudia just stood there. It would be nice to see Zoe flounder a little bit with a man who didn't fawn all over her. At twenty-five, she'd had one serious relationship that Claudia knew of, and it had ended badly. Her sister hadn't been interested since, and it would be nice to have someone to go through the angst of dating with.

"That's not an answer, Zoe. Fish impressions don't tell me anything, you know. Sputtering isn't pretty, either."

"It doesn't matter if he was cute or not. He's obnoxious."

"Which only tells me that you want him and don't want to want him for some reason." She turned back to the stovetop and gave the chicken a brisk stir. The sound of Justin stomping down the hallway from the back bedrooms put her on instant defensive alert. They were having a relatively good day so far, even with turning Nate down for dinner. Her offer of the batting cages tomorrow night was going a long way toward smoothing things out. But if Justin started asking about her love life again now that Edward was no more, she didn't know what she was going to say.

She wanted Nate but would definitely not tell her son that, since it would be his fondest dream come true.

There was so much between her and Nate, so many years of good friendship, and she didn't want to mess anything up. In her wildest dreams, though, she did want to ride the man straight into the sunset.

"That reason will not be discussed right now with your son coming out of his cave for dinner. If you're nice, I might tell you later."

With that, Zoe moved to the cabinets and started pulling out dishes and glasses. Putting them on the counter, she gave Justin the beady eye when he walked into the kitchen and threw himself into a chair.

"Okay, okay! Jeez. I'll set the table already."

Claudia leaned her forehead against the spice cabinet to the left of the stove. Normally he was a great kid, but something was bothering him lately, and she didn't know how to get him to talk about it, other than beating it out of him. He was his normal happy-go-lucky self most of the time, but they'd have moments when the attitude would come popping out like this. Wasn't the angsty stage supposed to come in a few years? Didn't she at least have until the teenage years to wait for the attitude and backtalk?

Zoe raised an eyebrow, and they shared a look. Yeah, she remembered being a mouthy ten-year-old, too.

So her mother's curse had come through with flying colors. She may have given birth to herself in male form and would have to endure the kind of teenager she had been. Sucked for her.

"Dinner's ready. Let's sit down and have a nice meal without the attitude, Justin. I'm not in the mood tonight."

"You're never in the mood for anything anymore. You probably won't even take me to the batting cages like you said. Nate would take me, if you'd let him."

"It's not Nate's job to watch you and keep you occupied all the time. He should be allowed to have a life of his own every once in a while, you know." Although that life could seriously change for the better, in her opinion, if his mission changed to trying to keep her happy. And if she could just figure out how to let him know she was interested, maybe that would be a possibility. But how do you tell the man who has seen you at your worst that you want him to think you're sexy? Especially when she couldn't even remember how to flirt properly?

She had been horrified to remember earlier that she had once even breastfed in front of him. There was no hope for her.

"Yeah, but Nate likes to spend time with me. And he'd spend even more if you'd stop going out on those stupid dates and just hang out with him and me."

For one insane second she almost asked if Nate had said anything about wanting to see more of her. Fortunately, she stopped herself before she'd even opened her mouth. "Just eat."

He munched and crunched his way through dinner, then got up as soon as he'd shoveled the last spoonful of peas into his mouth. "I'm going to play some video games."

"Is your homework done?"

"Yes, Mom. Yeesh." He tromped back down the hall much the way he'd come up it less than twenty minutes ago.

"Am I really that naggy of a mom?" Claudia asked, sitting with her elbow cocked on the table.

"Oh, sweetie, you remember what it was like at that age. I think the more important question is whether or not Nate has given Justin a reason to think your dates are dorky. Aside from them actually being dorky."

"I don't want to go there right now. I had a terrible afternoon trying to remember at least one time I'd been sexy in front of Nate over the last ten years. And the definitive answer was never. Other than going out on dates with other men and him seeing me when I came back in my flats from some date with a shorty, he hasn't seen me dressed up in forever. No wonder he thought I had something in my eye. I'm a failure as a woman."

"You are not! I don't ever want to hear you say that again." Zoe shoved back her chair and whisked plates off the table, going so far as to take Claudia's plate even though she was still trying to eat her chicken.

"Hey, do you mind bringing that back? I don't inhale my food the way you and the monster do."

Zoe at least had the grace to blush. "Sorry."

Plate back on the table in front of her, Claudia pushed it away, realizing that her appetite had vanished. "I'm just being dumb, anyway. There's no way a guy like Nate would want me when he has so many other women available to him. I have so much baggage I need my own valet."

"Don't say that, either. Everyone has something." Zoe moved toward the sink and Claudia couldn't see her face, but something in her voice was wrong.

"What's up? Are we back to the lawyer?"

"No, we're not back to the lawyer because I don't want to talk about him."

"Come on. It would give me something to think about other than the disaster my love life has turned into." Claudia got up and nudged Zoe over to the sink to fill it with water while she finished clearing the dishes of her completely uninspired meal.

"I just think men should be a little less like dogs, is all. And this guy is a major hound."

"But I thought you hadn't met him before today. I haven't even heard of him before this afternoon."

"Oh, I've heard of him, all right, and none of it good." Zoe threw a spatula into the dishwater and had suds splashing onto the front of her shirt and Claudia's. "Crap. Look at that. He even made me ruin my best T-shirt."

"Zoe, that T-shirt is older than Justin. I highly doubt you could ruin it at this point. And why are you so down on him?"

Zoe seemed to struggle with something internally. Then her shoulders slumped, and she sank her chin to her chest.

Tucking a finger under Zoe's chin, Claudia lifted her sister's face. "You know you can tell me anything."

"It's not a big deal. Let's just say that it sucks to find a man you would give all capital letters to and make him a MAN in your mind, and he turns out to have given something a little more substantial to five women in the last five weeks."

"Oh." Claudia let that process through her brain and got the rest of the dishes from the table, allowing Zoe to elaborate if she wanted to.

Apparently she wanted to. "Here's the thing. I've had this client I was just talking to May about today. I was bitching because he's sent five pretty big bouquets to five different women, one a week. I told her what an absolute beast he is and that I was really tempted to attach my own little note to the flowers telling the ladies to beware because they weren't the only one or even two." She wiped the back of her hand over her forehead to move some hair that had fallen forward. "Then I go into Uncle Al's office thinking I'm going to see my favorite guy, and instead come face to face with a serious hunk o' male who is totally drool worthy. I'm spinning fantasies—until I hear his name and realize it's the flower dog."

Claudia tried hard not to laugh. This wasn't funny, except that many things came easy to Zoe, and a little shake-up wasn't going to be the end of the world for her. "How can you know for sure it was him?"

Zoe slapped a hand into the water and grabbed more silverware to wash. "I can't wait to see you fall, and I mean seriously fall, for Nate. I am so going to enjoy the ride. And the reason I know is that no one else in town has a name like Dexter Zegray."

"That is true, I guess. Hmmm, Zoe Zegray. Has a nice ring to it."

Zoe slapped the water again, but this time she hit Claudia in the chest with the warm soapy water and the fight was on.

Later that night, though, Claudia couldn't help thinking about whether "Claudia West" also had a nice ring to it. She'd known Nate forever and yet had never written his and her names inside a heart in a notebook at school. Never wrote "Mrs. Claudia West" with a heart dotting the I. Never put their initials with the plus sign between. Never even considered him a real male. He had always just been her best friend. Why did she have to go and get all hormonal and lusty? What if she ruined everything?

Indecision was riding her back like a nasty monkey. Sure, she'd doubted herself time and again about what she was doing, if she was raising Justin right, what to wear to dinner. But she hadn't had this male/female indecision in a very long time. The old Claudia would have just gone for it, but she found this Claudia was more gun shy than she'd thought.

Finally, she fell asleep, only to dream of Nate in completely inappropriate places, doing decadent things. It started her morning off—right up until the point when she saw him working on the shop and could barely meet his eyes.

****

Nate whistled tunelessly as he removed a stack of mail from the odd-shaped box standing in front of his house Friday afternoon. He'd put in a hard day at Decadence, getting things blocked out and set up for the build-out Claudia wanted. He'd tried to catch her eye at the store in the morning, but she looked really busy and he hadn't pursued it. She had a lot on her mind with Peter here, and he didn't need her right away. He'd catch her tomorrow. He hoped she and Justin were getting along decently and the boy wasn't giving her any problems. He'd tried talking to Justin when the kid had walked by him on his way home from school, but as soon as he'd asked what was bothering the little guy, Justin had clammed up. Nate knew he'd wheedle it out of him eventually, maybe at dinner with Claudia next week. Or Claudia would tell him. Either way, he'd told Justin that his phone was always on. He and Justin hadn't ever talked about Peter, his biological father, but with the guy back in town and Justin's general moodiness of late, Nate had no doubt it would explode at some point. And he'd be there for him. Just like he was for Claudia, though she, too, had been acting weird lately. Must be all the stress, he thought.

A recent gag gift from his cousin, the mailbox made him laugh every time he saw it. Today was no exception as he took a good look at it and tried to push any concerns to the back of his mind. It was perfect. No one else in his circle of friends had an oversized replica of an Xbox Game System to hold mail.

"Hey there, sonny," a familiar masculine voice rumbled from behind him, and Nathan jumped. His next-door neighbor, Fred, erupted with his trademark laugh and continued, "I caught you off guard. Sorry about that, my boy."

Nate turned and beheld Fred in all his glory. There really wasn't another word for it. And smiled. No one Nate had ever met could compete with the outfits Fred managed to put together. Today it was a pair of green polyester slacks and a flamingo pink polo shirt.

"Well, it's a fine, beautiful day, isn't it?" Fred said, and his flash of blinding white teeth was proof positive of the wizardry of dentures.

"Yes, sir, it is," Nate replied. "And how are you feeling today?"

"Good as gold. Good as gold," Fred said. "Got myself a new girlfriend down at the club, and we're stepping out tonight. Me and my Edna."

Nate stifled a chuckle. Fred Watson didn't look a day over eighty-five, and he led a more social life than Nate did at the ripe old age of twenty-eight. But Nate had hopes that might change. And soon. There was a girl down at the bank he'd been thinking about asking out. Yeah, he had to remember the girl down at the bank and forget his wacky notions about Claudia flirting with him when she was probably just trying to handle this Peter situation as best she could.

"So, is this one a keeper, Fred?" Nate asked. If he remembered correctly, this was Fred's sixth girlfriend in the last eight months. Fred Watson, the aging Lothario, was an inspiration.

The dentures flashed again in a wide smile. "Well, now, son," Fred's voice dropped, as if he were imparting a secret. "They're all keepers. Even if it's only for a short time." And then he laughed uproariously at his own wit, his many chins jiggling merrily. "By the way, boy, when are you going to get a girl for yourself?" Fred asked as he peered at Nate from under bushy white eyebrows. "Got yourself this big house and don't have no family to share it with. Seems a shame to let that backyard of yours go to waste with just your flowers and your patio furniture."

Since Fred brought up Nate's lack of female companionship every time the two talked, Nate smiled again, devilishly this time, shrugged a shoulder, and gave his standard answer. "That's why I'm here, Fred.

I'm going to find myself a beautiful ski bunny or corn-fed girl and raise a whole passel of kids."

Hands folded over his round stomach, his neighbor laughed jovially, and his belly shook for long moments. Then Fred rearranged his face into a look of mock severity, his blue eyes still twinkling with mirth. "Gotta decide between one or the other, my boy. Can't have both, I don't think. Though times may be different. But see that you start soon, sonny. You're not getting any younger, you know." With that bit of sage advice, Fred began walking up the length of his driveway.

The words, coming from someone who was old enough to be his grandfather, really got Nate in the gut. For all he knew, Fred would get married for the third time before he could even manage to walk down the aisle once.

"Have a great time on your date this evening, Fred," Nate called as he watched the man who had been "advising" him since he was a snot-nosed kid running around with his friends on their skateboards. When this house had gone up for sale, Nate had been skeptical about living next to the old man, but it had turned out to be one of the best decisions of his life. "Keep an eye out for the ski bunnies for me."

"I always keep an eye out for the ski bunnies," Fred returned.

Nate saluted as Fred made his way back to his house, calling over his shoulder that he needed to get ready for his red-hot date at 4:30.

Fred was going to be right on time by Nate's watch. And that also meant Nate had the whole evening stretched out in front of him.

Logan had a date with some girl, and Claudia had

never picked up her phone when he tried to call this afternoon about Peter. His few close friends were on a slow-pitch baseball team together, and tonight was practice. He'd been asked to join but had turned them down because he'd wanted to be available if Justin needed him.

Okay, that was a little pathetic. Sure, he loved the little guy, but he didn't need to be a doormat. This kind of thing had only happened over the last year or so, when Justin had started freaking Claudia out. It was right after they had moved out of Claudia's mom's house and into their own apartment with Zoe.

Fortunately, the phone chose that moment to ring. At this point he'd gladly talk to a telemarketer to get his thoughts off the path they were strolling down.

But he didn't get there in time to answer. That just might have been divine intervention.

Because it wasn't a telemarketer. It was his mom. "Sweetie," she said in her harsh smoker's voice. "Call your mama and your grandma when you get a chance. We have something we want you to do for us. You know how your grandma is, so call right away or the biddy won't get off my back." It sounded like she turned away from the phone; her voice got muffled and distant. "Yes, I called you an old biddy. Please don't tell me you're going to be ornery in your old age. Christ!" Now back to him. "Yeah, yeah, love from me and the old bat. Oops." Then she laughed and hung up.

What a family. No wonder he'd never been in any huge hurry to invite anyone into it. Claudia and her whole crew from Zoe to May to Claudia's parents were there by default since they'd been around forever, but inviting someone new in was always something to think long and hard about. They'd have to deal with his mom and his grandma, who he was pretty sure was Fred's age, but, since every year her age went down a number or three, he could never be sure.

Stepping over some fallen toy soldiers and a handful of games spread out on the floor, Nate headed for the kitchen. He threw the mail on the table. The whole pile slid along the slick surface but stopped before completely falling off the table, joining others on the table. He wasn't normally a slob, but with two jobs going on, he was busy. He really needed to clean this place up, and tonight was the perfect time. Though he knew Claudia and Justin were probably at the batting cages, he didn't want to intrude. Justin seemed to have some stuff on his mind lately, and maybe he would talk to Claudia about it tonight in between swings.

For his part, Nate had no plans for the evening. It was still early, and he was going to be busy again come Monday. Especially since he was probably taking Claudia and Justin out to dinner Monday evening. It would be a welcome fun thing to do after the lunch they had to attend this weekend. He still hadn't decided whether he wanted to go or not.

Wandering over to the refrigerator, he pulled open the door and checked out what he had. He grabbed a package of filet he'd taken out of the deep freeze in the garage earlier in the week and seasoned it. He'd grill again. No big deal.

Thinking about the upcoming couple of days brought two things to the front of his mind. For one, he hoped Claudia could handle Peter. He knew she could, but he hoped she came out the other side okay. Secondly, as much as it was never a hardship to take

Claudia anywhere—she'd been potty trained for years—he did hope her nervous tick would go away before their dinner.

Then again, maybe she finally needed glasses. He'd been telling her for years that holding paper at arm's length wasn't the norm. And if she really wanted to enjoy those romance novels she liked to read, she should break down and get glasses. Maybe that was the problem the other night when her eyelashes kept fluttering.

Because the only other explanation he'd been able to come up with over the last few days was that she was trying to flirt with him, and that made about as much sense as using a ballpeen hammer to pound in a stake on a railroad tie. Not to mention they'd been friends forever and, despite a few wet dreams at night when he was younger, he'd put her in a box labeled Not For Sex, Ever.

It was too ridiculous to even contemplate. Wasn't it?

Chapter Four

"Come on, Justin," Claudia called down the short hallway, hoping to be heard over his stereo. Wasn't loud stereo noise supposed to come in the teens? Her child was smart for his age and sometimes older than she thought he should be, but he was really pushing this expected-behavior thing straight over a cliff.

"What?" the muffled reply came through the closed door near the end of the hallway.

"Come on out if you want to go to the batting cages." She pounded on the door for good measure.

"What?" A little louder this time.

"All right," she said to herself. "I've tried the whole respecting privacy business, but this is ridiculous." Turning the knob, she tried to shove open the door but something was in the way.

"Mom!" he said in a whiny, sing-song voice.

"Justin!" Claudia sent it right back to him. "Move whatever the heck is keeping this door wedged closed, and let me in."

"But this is my room, and you said you'd respect my privacy."

Ooh, it sucked to have her words thrown back at her, especially when she was trying to do something nice for the little hooligan, something she didn't even particularly like to do. "I wouldn't have any problem respecting your privacy if you could ever hear me."

"What?"

"Open the door!" She was trying so hard not to use the f-word right now, and her breath gurgled in the back of her throat. What a great way to spend a fun Friday night.

"Jeez, Mom, just hold on a second."

Oh, my God! She was not going to survive his puberty—and he might not either.

After much banging and grunting and groaning, the door opened. And it was like coming across an overflowing dumpster in the middle of a skating rink.

There, standing in the middle of piles of clothes, magazines, toys, and CDs, was her son. Four-foot-nine of attitude, maleness, and angst. But under it all, he was a great kid, one who tried to cook her dinner and would rub her back when she'd had a long day. One who still to this day made Mother's Day and Father's Day cards for her. One who really was the apple of her eye when he wasn't being a pain in her ass.

She propped herself against the door jamb and waited for him to stop shuffling his feet and actually look at her. She didn't have long to wait, and she got a half-cocked smile, one that was pure Nate. It forced her a half step back as it rocked her in her shoes.

When had Justin become a small Nate and no longer a small Claudia, or even a small Peter? In the looks department, Justin and Nate couldn't be farther from each other. Justin was the spitting image of Peter with his dark hair and dark eyes. But in attitude and mannerisms, he was a little Claudia and a lot Nate.

Was she going after the right thing with wanting Nate for herself? What if she broke the friendship and the easy relationship her son had with the one man in his life who had accepted him from day one, with the exception of his granddad on her side?

But then the half smile bloomed into a full-blown one, showing all his pearly whites and the eye tooth that was still growing in, and he was all Justin. A little con artist who could charm the money out of his grandma's pocketbook.

"So what did you want to tell me, Mom? I'm all ears for you now." He patted her shoulder and weaseled his way under her arm to lean against her side. "Are you still going to take me to the batting cages? Because that would be so cool. You would be the best mom ever. Not that you aren't right now the best mom ever, but then you'd be the bestest, *bestest* mom ever, and I could brag to all the guys about what a great mom I have." He even had the audacity to wink at her.

"You're laying it on a little thick, don't you think, kid?"

"Aw, shucks. Of course not. You know I mean every word of it."

"Aw, shucks? Now I know you're laying it on thick, like crap in a backed-up sewage system."

"Mo-om!"

It was a true pleasure to gross him out. "Anyway, yes, I am taking you to the batting cages if you'd get your stuff together and get some shoes on."

He dashed around his room faster than she'd seen him move in a while. A moment later he was in the hallway with the smile, a comic book, and some dubious shoes on his feet.

"I thought I threw those sneakers away last week."

"I saw them in the trash and figured they'd been dumped by accident, so I took them back out. They only kind of smell like bananas now."

They were high-top Converse, had about ten holes in the fabric of each shoe, and drawings all over the canvas. There was a reason they had been in the trash, and it wasn't an accident. But she'd learned to pick her battles, and right now the battle she wanted to have was the one about the music, not his footwear choice.

He seemed to listen as she talked about the noise level of the music and how it was disruptive to the shop downstairs as well as making it hard for her to hear him and vice versa. He seemed to take it all in, nodding at the appropriate places, and then proceeded to crank up the stereo in the car and sing at the top of his lungs.

Maybe she would take him on about the shoes.

****

Sixty minutes and about three hundred balls later, Claudia wasn't capable of taking on anyone about anything. She'd gladly sleep on top of those shoes if the choice were given to her.

"Come on, Mom. No time for sitting down and resting. You're not old. You should have more energy than this." He swung his bat a couple of times, warming up inside the cage, and then readjusted his helmet.

"You didn't say I had to hit balls, too." She sat behind the fence, willing to risk permanent chain linking on her cheek if she could just rest her eyes for a single minute.

She was pathetic. An hour of swinging a bat shouldn't take this much out of her. But she hadn't exercised in forever, and her demon spawn of a child had set her up with fast pitch for about three rounds before she realized other people had slower speeds, where the ball wasn't aimed and determined to take out a leg or arm or other valuable and necessary body part.

"Come on, this is fun!"

The chink of the bat striking the ball made her lift her head a fraction. "Good hit." Then her chin dropped to her chest again, and she admitted defeat. Sure, being the bestest, *bestest* mom was something to strive for, but this was ludicrous, and she was now sweaty beyond belief. She'd kill for a shower right before the small nap. She could do wonders with the water fountain on the other side of the cages, and the hard, standard-issue metal bench was looking downright cozy.

"Hey, batter, batter, swing, batter, batter!"

The voice was so familiar, and it sent tingles right down the center of her limp spine.

****

Nate hadn't had anything else to do tonight. After making his steak on the grill and trying to get interested in a DVD, he gave up and left the house. He'd felt lonely knowing even Fred was out on a Friday night. He'd thought about calling up his brother or a buddy, but spending time with his favorite guy and friend trumped any other plans he could have come up with.

So here he was, figuring Justin had had enough time to talk to his mom if he'd needed to and hoping he wasn't busting in on the poor little guy's parade.

Claudia jumped from her previous slumped position to sitting rigid in a hurry. He walked up behind her and automatically started kneading her shoulders. "Long day?"

"Mmmm. You have no idea." She purred and stretched.

He dropped his hands like she was a wire and they'd forgotten to turn off the electricity before stripping it bare.

"Is that all I get?" She looked up at him through lowered lashes, and he worried she might start in with the eyelash thing again.

"Yeah, well, I was just over this way and saw your car, so I thought I'd stop in and see how you were doing." He smiled and took a seat next to her. She was sweaty and dirty and looked like the Claudia he used to chase around the playground in elementary school. This was the more comfortable Claudia. The one he could deal with on a daily basis. He'd been crazy to think she had been flirting with him the other night.

Justin started packing his batting bag in the cage in front of them. Claudia moved her body a little on the bench to make room for Justin to sit down when he came out. But instead of moving down away from Nate, she moved toward him and ended up nearly smooshing her very curvy body up against his.

He popped off the bench like a jack-in-the-box. She nearly fell on the ground, righting herself at the last second.

"Are you okay?" he asked, grabbing her arm and fighting embarrassment. What the hell was wrong with him? "God, I'm so sorry."

"Not a problem, Nate." She lowered her lashes and fluttered them.

On second thought, what the hell was wrong with her?

Cool fingers trailed up his arm and lightly pinched his bicep. "Why so nervous?"

Good question, but he didn't feel he had a good answer. She was running him ragged. Time to take control back and get onto a different subject. He could still feel the imprint of her breast on his arm where she'd leaned against him. And as much as he'd like to say it hadn't affected him in the least—come on, this was his friend Claudia—a boner was starting in his pants. A completely inappropriate response to the girl whose ponytails he used to pull and whose shoes he had put slugs in.

"I'm not nervous. I, um, just remembered I need to get to the grocery store before they close."

"But it's only six-thirty. You have hours. I was thinking maybe we could get some pizza and a movie and close ourselves in for the night." She leaned back against the bench with her arms behind her, crossed her legs and seemed to thrust out her chest.

He almost swallowed his tongue. He found it tucked into the side of his mouth between his teeth and unstuck it so he could say, "Tonight's not going to work for me, but I'll definitely see you Sunday at the Peter lunch. Have a good night." He scooted out of there so fast his pants might have been on fire. That description was not too far from the truth he realized as he sat in his car telling his libido to calm the hell down.

****

"Now when you go near him again, you might not want to revert to the blinking thing again." Two hours later, the lesson had begun. While Claudia groaned at her sister's words, Zoe was obviously relishing every single syllable coming out of her mouth. It wasn't often she got to be the one telling her older sister what to do and how to do it. There was a reason for that.

Apparently Zoe's date had not gone off well, and so she had come back to the apartment to corner Claudia, who was alone for the night. After Nate had left for his mysterious and ridiculous errand to the grocery store, one of the moms of Justin's baseball teammates had found them at the batting cages and invited him for a sleepover. Even though the night stretched out before her, Claudia had said yes. Honestly, it would be nice to have a night off to regroup after Nate had turned her down for dinner and a movie in. She needed to lick her wounds, and instead she was getting flirting tips from Zoe.

"It wasn't a blinking thing! I was trying to bat my eyelashes at him."

She demonstrated, and Zoe jumped right on her. "Honey, that is not batting your eyelashes. That it definitely blinking like you have something in your eye."

Claudia heaved a sigh. "I told you I was a complete lost cause. Even at the batting cages I couldn't get it right. He talked to Justin and then just walked away as if I didn't exist except as the mom."

"No, no, no. I'm just saying we might need to take a more direct approach. After all these years, he may not get a more subtle hint."

"I'm going to give up on it. I don't know why I thought I could flirt anyway. We're comfortable the way we are. Forget about it."

As if.

"I will not forget about it. You want that cake, finally, and we're going to get it for you. Maybe even cake with icing! We are not giving up."

"I wish I had your enthusiasm. I think all I'll ever be is a mother. I don't even know how to be a woman anymore. And I just want the cake. I'll never actually find the icing."

Apparently, Zoe thought that line of thinking needed to be nipped right in the bud.

"I was right there along with you when you were getting bigger and bigger with your pregnancy. Hell, I even had odd cravings right along with you, at the ripe old age of fifteen. I am not going to let you shrivel up and die an old maid at twenty-eight. Life is not over. We'll nail this, and then you'll be the happiest woman in the world."

"Or I'll nail Nate and have no more best friend. I don't know if I still even remember how to have sex." Claudia threw her hand over her brow and leaned back against the kitchen counter.

Zoe grabbed her hand and pinched her finger. "Do not go all drama queen on me. Now, let's get started so we can get you laid and happy. Time's a-wasting, and I don't have any more of it to go out and buy you blue and green streamers for your poor-me party."

"You have never been funny, and I don't know why you continue to try. I'm being serious here, and you're mocking me."

"I'm not mocking you." Zoe sat at the kitchen table and retrieved a notepad from under the jumble of crap that had accumulated there throughout the week. It seemed like it was the one place everyone dropped their stuff. Justin's socks, Claudia's purse and mail, Zoe's jacket, all mounded on the table like a trash heap gone bad.

"You are." At the wooden table, Claudia pulled out the chair across from Zoe and plopped into it. "You think this is easy after so many years? Nate has seen me breastfeed my kid and cry all over him when Justin did something unbearably cute or horribly wrong. Why is he going to want this?" She waved a hand at her less-than-perfect body and then pulled some of her long hair away from her head.

"I think Nate has wanted that since he was sixteen years old."

"Yeah, and at sixteen I weighed forty pounds less and had highlights shining in my perfect hair."

"You also fixed your bangs in a fan that stood about five inches above your forehead."

Claudia thunked her head on the hard wood of the table. "Don't remind me. This is useless."

"All right, that's the last time you're allowed to say that. I've given you time to be a sad sack, but no more. We're going to do this, and we're going to do it right. Once Nate gets a clue, he'll fall right into your clutches." Zoe made note of the highlights on her pad and added a few ideas about how to go about making Nate even more besotted than he already was. When Claudia tried to get a better peek at the paper, Zoe slapped a hand on top of the pad.

"And what about you?"

Zoe's head whipped up and she zeroed in on Claudia with narrowed eyes. "Nothing about me. This is all you." She doodled a heart on the page under the word "manicure" and avoided looking at Claudia.

"Then I guess you don't have any problem with the fact Dexter Zegray called and wants you to come in to go over some additional suggestions?"

"Sure. Not a problem. I'll go see him next week."

Trying to force Zoe to change the subject was not helping. Claudia was going to have to either buck up and do this or get rid of Zoe, and the getting rid of thing was not looking promising.

"I don't even know why we're discussing flirting with Nate, much less trying to sleep with him. I don't want him to see me as some hussy." Claudia rose from her seat and fussed with the knob of the silverware drawer to the left of her hip. "Besides, it's not going to work, and I don't want to waste any time doing ridiculous things. I have that luncheon Sunday at May's house."

"Oh, no, you're not getting out of it that easily, sister dear. I spent time making this list, and I'm not going to throw it away simply because you're getting cold feet. Now sit down, and let's get moving."

What followed was too agonizing to describe. Claudia would have nightmares for years about making kissy faces at herself in the mirror and turning her head just right so her hair fell over her shoulder. And in the end she only felt like more of a failure. Not that she'd tell Zoe that, if she valued her sanity.

She went to bed counting down the hours until she could see Peter and get him out of her hair. If she seriously wanted to pursue Nate, she would have to do it her own way.

****

"Emergency girl meeting," Claudia called out the next morning as she streamed through the front door of Decadence with her heart racing and her palms damp.

May looked up from her kneeling position in front of a dress dummy covered in silk. Pins dangled from between her lips, and her hair was up in a sloppy bun.

Claudia kept on toward the back, knowing May would follow close behind, pins or no pins. Zoe called out she'd be right there after she stuck something in the refrigerator.

When Zoe showed up, she grabbed one of the other chairs from the wall and pulled it in close, then took Claudia's left hand in hers. May did the same thing with the last chair and her right hand.

"What's going on?" they said in stereo.

"Nate just called, and he has the plans for Decadence ready. He said he wanted to come over and go through them with me, but I can't do it. I need one of you to stand in for me."

"Absolutely not," Zoe said, while May sat with a smile on her face.

"Why is it absolutely not? I've done plenty for you. You could do this one thing for me. And, May, you can stop smiling. I believe you just pulled the friendship card the other day about this lunch tomorrow. I can't do this knowing that he might know I'm attracted to him but he's too nice to tell me it's not going to happen. He completely turned me down for dinner and a movie at home the other night, just to go grocery shopping!"

"Don't be so difficult, Claudia," Zoe said. "You're trying to look for reasons not to get involved with a man you find attractive but are afraid to test the waters with."

But what if that fear was very valid and could end the most important relationship in her and her son's life? "That's fine for you to say."

"And what's that supposed to mean?"

"It means you don't even date seriously. How can you be any judge?"

"I date, and that's not the point."

May leaned back in her chair and rolled her eyes. Claudia caught the motion and gave her a sharp look. "I'm just saying you don't have much experience to go on other than being a serial dater. You haven't exactly got a track record for long-term commitments."

"Again, so not the point. The point is that you are ready to finally give the guy who's lusted after you for years a chance to once and for all convince you he could be more than a friend. Don't screw it up by hiding."

Claudia's heart stuttered as she frowned. That might be all too true, but there was more at stake here than just riding the baloney pony. This was her life.

"I'm sorry," Zoe said. "That didn't come out the way I'd meant it to. And I know this is probably hard for you."

Claudia sat back, but she didn't roll her eyes like May had. Instead, tears welled up and threatened to spill over. "You think this is easy for me? I just realized the other day that I haven't been out with a truly interesting man since I was a teenager. Not only that, but I only have your word to go on that Nate is interested in me."

"And mine," May said, popping into the conversation. "I know he's held a torch for years, at least since you were in eleventh grade."

"No way!" Claudia leaned forward in her chair and grabbed May's hands. "No way has he wanted me that long without talking about it."

"Yes way," Zoe answered, before May could. "You've just been blind. Like having a child took away your ability to see what's going on right beneath your nose." Zoe put her hands on top of May's and Claudia's. "Sweetie, why else do you think he's stuck around for all these years and done so much for you?"

Claudia sat back in her chair, crossing her legs and

hugging her arms tight to her stomach. "Because we've been friends for years."

"I won't discount that, seriously. But why hasn't he found someone for himself, then? Why does he continue to come to our house and watch Justin? Or coach his team? Have me make you flowers on your birthday? I've had male friends, and they never did even one of those things, much less all of them."

"Maybe I have been looking at it wrong."

"Maybe you have," May said. "He doesn't say anything specific about you, but I can tell."

"I think you need to embrace what you want, Claudia, and decide how you're going to go out and get it done." May flipped her hair back over her shoulder and out of her face. "You need to go get him, no holds barred, the way I did with Brad."

A wistful expression flitted across May's face. One Claudia wanted to see on her own face in the mirror instead of the kissy lips. Before she had time to think about what that would look like, the bell rang over the door and their mother announced her entrance.

"Hi!" Mona waved from the cake counter where she was snitching a small sample.

"Mom, those are for the customers." Claudia walked away from the emergency girl meeting and snatched the rest of the plate out of her mother's hands. After putting the domed plate back into the display case, she rested her hands on her hips.

"Oh, posh! I was in the area and hankering for some of your delicious sugary stuff, so I stopped in to see what was going on, now that I'm loosening up my schedule some." She zeroed in on Zoe, who flinched. "You did get that information for me, right? How long is this going to take?"

"Yeah, it's all taken care of and the ball is rolling, Mom."

"Yes, Mom," Claudia said, winking at May. "All taken care of and wrapped in a pretty bow by a man named Dex, who has caught dear Zoe's eye." That ought to show Zoe and deflect any interest in Claudia. Plus, it was exactly what sisters were for, butting in where they weren't needed.

Zoe retaliated immediately. "Did I tell you Claudia's trying to figure out how to hook up with Nate?"

It spiraled down from there, with May laughing and Mona probing her daughters for all the information. Zoe, of course, gave as little as she could, continuing to deflect everything onto Claudia.

"We're not dating," Claudia said for the fifth time.

"Well, you should be. It's a good thing you finally woke up to what a pony that Edward was. I can't believe you went out with him."

Claudia didn't know whether to laugh or cry that her mom also thought Edward was a pony, or even knew what that reference meant. She tackled the one thing she could. "You're the one who set us up."

"Oh, lordy, girl, that was only to get you to open your eyes to see what a man Nate was. I kept hoping you'd get a clue, but when you never did, I was starting to despair."

Claudia did an impression of a carp, like Zoe's from the other night, until her mom gently closed her mouth for her and waved goodbye. She was going to miss having her mom in the shop on a permanent basis, but it would be good for her parents to spend time together, now they were both retired. They'd earned the right to take some leisure time. Maybe she should talk to Zoe about sending them on a cruise. Or she'd talk to Zoe about that once she stopped giving her sister the evil eye and the cold shoulder.

Zoe deliberately stood in Claudia's way when she came back from putting a cake into the big refrigerator in the back. Claudia tried to step around her, but Zoe just moved with her. "You're not getting away from me. After this I can bug you all night upstairs in the apartment. I'll be like a burr on your butt."

Claudia cracked a slight smile she tried to shut down immediately. "You are a burr on my butt anyway. What's new about that?"

"Oh, you're a real comedian, but I can see you want to smile. I know you do. You want to smile, don't you? Come on."

"Oh, all right, you pain in the ass. I'll smile, but I'm still not happy you tried to throw me to the wolf. I have half a mind to go give her a call and see if she and Uncle Al can work on getting you and Dex together."

"Please don't. You know how she gets. One grandchild isn't enough for her, and I don't want to get either the third degree or the major maternal encouragement, otherwise known as 'push.' I promise not to mention one more thing about Nate to her. Let's shake on it. We'll leave her out of everything. In fact, it may not be that hard to do, since she and Dad should be spending a bunch of time together and she won't be in here every day."

Claudia stuck out her hand. "No spitting, though. I can keep a promise without exchanging bodily fluids."

"But would you want to if I were Nate?"

"You're not Nate, so that's not a valid question. Besides, I'm still hung up on what exactly I want there. I saw him yesterday, and he barely looked at me. I don't know what I'm doing wrong. Now I have to go sit with him over blueprints when he is completely oblivious to my charms, what few there are."

"May told you you're going to have to be blunt with him. It's been a lot of years, and he's not going to know what you're doing—or won't believe it even if he thinks it."

Claudia blew out a sigh that lifted her bangs. "Well, that just sucks. He should get a clue, so I don't have to give him one." She leaned on the top of her counter, messing with a trail of ivy decorating a fake display cake. "Does this ever get any easier?"

"Unfortunately, I have no idea, as you and May so nicely pointed out to me earlier at the emergency meeting. Now go upstairs, make sure all Justin's dirty underwear is put away, and vamp yourself out. I'll pick Justin up from his friend's and get us some lunch. That should give you enough time to convince Nate of your interest."

****

Nate shifted from foot to foot outside Claudia's door, hesitating to go in now that he'd arrived. He heard noise inside the apartment, and the light eastern breeze played with the sheer curtains she'd put up a year ago. It was a welcoming home, one he liked to come to and hang out at. He felt a part of something there, even if it was just as a friend.

And they were just friends. Had been since they were in kindergarten. And then in each other's pockets from the time they were twelve and Claudia had started trying out recipes on him. He'd choked down the first few cakes because he'd really liked her. Just as he was about to have to tell her the truth or risk his stomach lining, she'd gotten better at what she was doing. Thank God. That was also about the time his hormones had started kicking in and he'd realized she was a girl.

What a mess he'd made of things when he'd tried to give her a kiss the first time, the first time for both of them. He'd never forget the complete bafflement on her soft face when he'd come at her, eyes open and lips pursed. She ended up laughing, and he'd forced himself to laugh with her.

He was wasting time standing out here and reminiscing. He had the plans for her remodel of Decadence under his arm and a solid reason for being at her house. Procrastination wasn't going to do anything but draw things out.

He knocked, though he really didn't have to anymore. Claudia had told him on more than one occasion to just walk on in. But a part of him, the very male part, still feared girl rituals and what he might accidentally interrupt.

"Come on in," Claudia's muffled voice said through the door.

He straightened his shirt, smoothed his hair, and checked his pants before opening the door. He realized he'd need to pull his shirt down a little farther to cover his jeans, and he held the plans over his crotch. Dammit. He couldn't exactly stand out here thinking about the exact measurements of his next build-out or what he planned on making for dinner to try to make his erection subside before he walked in. He was stuck.

He must have taken too long, because Claudia

came and opened the door herself, looking good enough to lick with her blonde hair pulled into a messy bun on the back of her head and skewered with a pencil. She should be illegal, plain and simple.

"Oh, hey!" she said dragging him in by the arm. "Zoe and Justin just went out to grab some subs while we go over the plans. They should be back soon."

Which meant they were all alone in the house, and he was semi-hard. But at least her eyelashes weren't fluttering. The other day at the batting cages must have been a figment of his overactive imagination. She was not into him, had never been into him, no matter how much he had wanted her, that one brief time in his youth.

While he'd been thinking all these ludicrous thoughts, she'd stepped in closer. Her hand brushed the front of his jeans when she took the plans from him. He jerked and tried to step out of the way. How was he going to hide anything now? He guessed he could make a mad dash for the kitchen table and take a seat to avoid showing his rampant evidence of wanting her. This was very uncomfortable and unfortunate. It shouldn't be happening right now. What in the hell had gotten into him?

Coward that he was, he fast-walked his way to the table and left her in the doorway to do whatever she would. He could have sworn he heard a snicker behind him, but maybe it was his mind messing with him.

Regardless, he sat at the table facing forward and staring at the stove directly in front of him. He focused on the house he would be working on next week, mentally listing the supplies he'd need to buy, hoping he could get his woody to deflate before he had to stand up again.

He waited for what felt like an eternity before he heard her footsteps. As she passed him, a whiff of something exotic and warm hit his nose. It made a joke of all his progress in getting his body to settle down. Claudia had always smelled pleasantly of Claudia, but this afternoon her scent was something entirely different.

And if he didn't want to swallow his tongue and not be able to talk like a normal human being, he needed to get his mind out of her pants and into the plans in her hand. Plans for what, he couldn't say right now. But maybe it would come back to him once she sat across from him and spread out the papers on the surface of the big kitchen table.

His heart nearly stopped in his too-warm chest when she spread the papers out while caging him between her arms. Her breasts rested against his back, electrifying his skin under his thin T-shirt. It flashed through his mind to stand up and get away, but she'd effectively cut off his escape route, unless he was willing to knock her backward.

He struggled to keep silent his groan at the feel of her body pressed up against his. God, it was like being a teenager all over again. He was impossibly hard and hoping his cock wouldn't knock on the underside of her table.

And then she started speaking. Right into his ear in a breathy voice that set the hair on the back of his neck standing on end. "Oh, Nate! These are fantastic."

He breathed in another lungful of that exotic scent and nearly choked. Maybe it would be better to just not breathe at all. He didn't know if he could last another ten seconds without exploding. "Thanks."

"I can't believe you were able to get everything drawn up and finished so quickly. I knew there was a reason I loved you so much." She squished herself down on his back, and he felt every line and softness of her body. He also felt her rigid nipples poke into his back.

To hell with not knocking her back. He had to stand up. Now. Damn the consequences. Not to mention the tent in his pants. He scooted back gently from the table. "I should—"

Before he could say any more, she lifted her hands from the table and wrapped them around his torso, shifting herself to fit the curve of his back and giving him a huge hug. This was unbearable.

He placed his hands over hers to pull them away, but his body had other ideas. He shifted back into her embrace, enjoying it in a way he shouldn't. They'd hugged numerous times, but this was different, and he didn't know how he felt about it.

He had no time and no desire to explore those feelings right now. His heart thumped so hard in his chest he was afraid she could hear it. He forced a laugh he didn't feel and followed through with his earlier intent to remove her hands. Turning to look at her, he prepared to tell her how much her enthusiasm meant to him and then get the hell out of there as fast as his legs could carry him without damaging his goods permanently. He needed breathing room—without essence of Claudia and spice filling the air. He needed room to get his distance back into place where it belonged. He needed to have his head checked for wanting her as more than a friend and feeling a faint kicking in his stomach that told him to go for it already.

But she took the option completely out of his hands when she grabbed his ears and laid a kiss on his lips like nothing he'd ever experienced before. For sure, there was no laughing going on this time.

Chapter Five

Nate's lips were infinitely softer than Claudia had ever dreamed. Her hands roamed his back, then clasped around his neck, pulling him down to her level. She rubbed her lips back and forth against his, electrified by finally being this close to him and planting one on him. Not to mention the fact that she'd actually gathered the courage to do what she'd wanted to do from the moment she opened the door.

He hadn't opened his mouth yet, but she was working on it by tracing the outline of his lips with her tongue. He made a noise in his throat that shot thrills right to her stomach, and she topped it with her own, "Mmmmmm."

And then she was cold, her arms empty, her heart stuttering. Her breath stopped in her lungs as she listened to the door slam closed behind him.

When it opened again, she was sitting in a straight-backed chair, elbows holding down his drawings on the table.

"I tried to take a little longer, but the monkey caught on that something was going on," Zoe called out as she waltzed by, food in hand. "He's coming up right now. I made him carry a few things so I could check out the scene and make sure he wouldn't walk in on something that would haunt him for years and be burned on the back of his eyelids forever."

Claudia would have laughed if she didn't feel so dejected. She heard cabinets opening and closing around her, and Zoe's footsteps quick and light. Then total silence descended for a second before the heavy tread of Justin's step sounded in the living room.

Zoe grabbed Claudia's chin and turned her head. "We'll talk later," she said, giving Claudia a one-armed hug. "For right now, you need to come up with a reason why Nate isn't here, while putting on your happy-mom face. Quick, before Justin trundles in."

Claudia did her best, knowing it wasn't enough. She told her lips to lift on the edges and form a smile, but they weren't listening. She'd made a mess of things, and now she had no idea how to make the situation any better.

But then Justin came stumbling into the kitchen under the weight of three big bags. Claudia couldn't help but laugh. "Think you loaded him up enough, Zoe?"

"I can carry it all," came his muffled reply from behind the white paper bags.

She got up from the table, the smile staying in place all on its own. "Let me at least help you set them down." She took the fragrant sacks and placed them on the table. Pulling food from each, she marveled at the amount of food Zoe had purchased. "Since when are we feeding an army?"

"Well, I wasn't sure what all to get, so I got a little of everything. It's not like we can't have leftovers. But we should eat the subs first. We can have lasagna for dinner tomorrow."

"Or I could have Derek over," Justin said, throwing himself into a chair. "I bet we could eat everything without a single problem."

Claudia ruffled his hair, knowing full well how much he hated the gesture. But they were going through a relatively smooth period, and she figured he could stand a little riling. "No friends tonight. We have a big day tomorrow."

"Yeah, but you got to have Nate over. Why is it always different for kids?"

Which brought the incident and the kiss crashing back to her. The smile dropped from her lips in an instant.

Justin was completely oblivious as he looked around the room as if he thought Nate was hiding in one of the cupboards or under the table. "Where is Nate, anyway?"

So it was time for her excuse that she hadn't even thought of yet. "Um, he ended up having to leave early."

"Damn, I wanted to ask him something," Justin said, pulling a sub over to his placemat.

"Hey!" Claudia said, once she found her tongue again. "We do not use language like that in this house."

"I heard Aunt Zoe say it yesterday when her show was a rerun."

Claudia turned her glare briefly to Zoe before zeroing back in on her son. "Regardless of Aunt Zoe's potty mouth, we do not use that word here. You know better."

"Fine." He waved her away with one hand while he used the other to cram half the sandwich into his mouth.

"It's not fine. I don't want to hear that word out of you again." Claudia sat back down, feeling that this was the last thing she needed right now.

He barely chewed his meat, bread, and cheese before swallowing. "All right, all right. I won't say it again, but I wanted to ask Nate something, and now he's not here. That..." He trailed off and slid a glance at Claudia from the corner of his eye. She knew what was coming and tried not to groan. "...sucks."

"I said you can only use that word in the appropriate context. Don't test me tonight. Why don't you just cram the rest of the hoagie in your mouth and zip it?"

He smiled at her with a mischievous gleam in his eye. "Okay."

She knew thinking the matter was over was too good to be true, but after the Nate debacle, she didn't have the energy to deal. So she changed the subject while she watched in horror as the other half of the sandwich really did disappear into his mouth in seconds. She shook her head. "Nice, Justin. Now what did you have to ask Nate?"

"Nothing," he mumbled. But at least he chewed this mouthful and a half.

"Okay." She knew what battles to pick and choose. If it was something really important, her son would tell her. She wasn't going to worry about it.

Zoe plopped down at the table and bit into her own sandwich. Apparently conversation was over for the next little while. Claudia took the opportunity to eat her own sandwich, thinking it didn't matter if she had the onions at this point; she'd already messed up her chances with Nate. Kissing would probably never happen again, since she'd botched it so completely. It had been almost as awkward as when he'd tried to give her their first kiss. At least then she'd had a lack of experience to hide behind. She had nothing this time. She hoped, though, that he wouldn't avoid her after this. This was exactly what she'd been worried about when she first thought about making him her cake. Damn Zoe for putting it into her head that Nate wanted her and had simply been waiting for her. And thank goodness she'd only said that in the confines of her head.

She glanced over at Justin to see him still chewing, and took another bite of her own dinner. He'd come out with it soon. She just hoped it wasn't too late to make sure Nate would be there when Justin needed him. Or at the very least that she hadn't messed things up so badly that he wouldn't take their calls.

****

Nate sat in his garage, inside his car, long after the overhead light for the garage door opener turned itself off. What the hell had happened in Claudia's apartment, and what did it mean?

The engine was off and the only noise was the intermittent knocking of his cooling engine. Closing his eyes, he inhaled the scent of old French fries in his car and couldn't help seeing again the scene that kept flashing across his brain.

Claudia's lips had settled on his, and her hands had locked around the back of his neck. He'd done his best not to step into her and take everything he could, everything she might have been offering. It felt wrong to be that close to her, and yet so right—in a bunch of ways.

What was she doing, anyway? Was this her acting out over Edward being an ass? Why would she have tried to kiss him? And there was no mistaking that it had been a kiss. It hadn't been an accident, but he had no idea why she was trying herself out on him.

He thumped his head against the back of his seat and wondered what the living hell was wrong with him. It would mess up everything they had between them for his long-ago crush to flare up now and ruin the way things were. He groaned in frustration, trying to ignore the fact that his pants were still way too tight.

And it was a crush—he was almost sure. He'd thought about her over the years and wondered what it would be like for them to be together. He was a man, after all. He always shut down that kind of thinking as soon as it started, though, since it was pointless and frustrating. It would never happen, and most of the time he didn't even want it to happen, since it would change their friendship from comfortable, and always there, to possibly volatile and probably unmanageable. Not to mention completely over if it didn't work out.

The knocking of the engine stopped. Complete silence enveloped him, and he realized he was getting cramped just sitting in the car, not moving, with his head pressed back and his pants straining at the seams.

He got out of the car and slammed the door behind him. Jamming the key into the lock on the door leading into the kitchen, he barely resisted twisting the metal hard enough to break it off in the unoffending lock. All he wanted was to live a simple life and hang out with Claudia, hang out with her kid, who was funny and a kick to be around. Do his construction work and come home every day to eat and sleep, and get up to do it all again the next day.

Sure, it might not seem like the most exciting life, but he was fine with that. In fact, he preferred it to the way things used to be before he moved out of his parents' house and got his own, with its peace and quiet. He liked being able to go out and do things and still be able to come home to silence if that was what he wanted.

He entered the kitchen, and that silence seemed to sit on his chest like a two-by-four. It pressed in on him from all sides and breathed down his neck with huffing gasps. The house was dark and would stay that way until he turned on lights. It would stay quiet until he turned on the stereo or flicked on the TV or rattled pots and pans in a kitchen that wasn't nearly as warm or welcoming as the one in Claudia's apartment two miles away. It lacked the life and vitality of said apartment that was half the size of his place.

"Dammit!" He threw his keys onto the counter and reached for the light switch. But with his hand hovering over the switch plate, he hesitated. He stood there frozen.

Had he already thrown something away by not responding to Claudia? Did she think he didn't want her because he'd run like a coward? What exactly did she want from that kiss?

He had tried to put it down to hormones, or possibly Peter being back, as he drove home. Why else would she have kissed him when she never had before? But then he thought about the fluttering eyelashes from the other day and her getting so close to him over the last few days. Was there a message there that he had totally been deliberately missing? And if there was, what on earth was he going to do about it?

****

The dreaded Sunday had come. It had occurred to

Claudia that morning that she should probably prepare Justin for meeting his biological father for the first time. She had avoided the thought for the last several days, hoping she wouldn't actually have to do anything. But now that the day had arrived, she was going to have to address the subject. Damn.

Because she tried to learn her lesson after Justin's whining from Friday about her not respecting his privacy in his room, Claudia knocked on his bedroom door. He'd better answer it quick, or his whole bid for privacy was going to go out the window, along with about twenty of his favorite games.

"Coming!" he yelled. Why the child had to do everything at maximum volume was beyond her.

He opened the door without having to yank it through a ton of trash on his floor. This made her absurdly pleased, but most likely today was going to be one of those days where you took what you could get and cherished it like gold, even if it was only a lump of coal.

"Hey, Mom! What's up?" He was still in his pajamas but looked cheery. Another thing she would gladly take.

"It's going to be time to get ready soon. Remember, we have that lunch at Aunt May's house today. I want you in your good clothes, not a holey T-shirt." Leaning against the doorjamb, she tried to be inconspicuous about her roaming eyes as she took in his relatively clean room. Well, that might be a little too optimistic. How about his not-as-messy room? "Wear the button-down shirt and a clean pair of jeans, at least."

"Can I wear my Converses?"

Ugh. She really wanted to say no, since the things should have stayed in the trash where she'd put them last week, but was it worth the fight? Probably not. "Fine, but make sure the shirt is tucked in."

"Okay," he said as he began closing the door in her face.

She put her palm against the wood, keeping it open. "I think we should talk for a few minutes."

His smile drooped a little around the corners. "Why?"

"Because I think we should. Now, do you want to do this in your room?" She suppressed a shudder. "Or can you come out into the living room for a sec?"

"I guess I'll come out to the living room," he said, grudgingly.

There was nothing like a grudging consent to get a difficult conversation off on the right foot.

Zoe must have been lurking in the kitchen, because she emerged with three cups of hot chocolate and a plate of toast. "I thought we'd get the day started right, since it might not continue to go that way."

"Not helping," Claudia said under her breath so only Zoe could hear her.

"But I'm trying. Doesn't that get me brownie points? Plus, I promised to be on my best behavior today, and hot chocolate with dunking toast will go a long way toward that goal."

Claudia sighed. Truthfully, she had been hoping to do this without Zoe's interference. Of course, she could ask her sister to leave, but it wouldn't accomplish anything. And she'd known there would be more than just herself in charge when she decided to move into this home with her sister instead of striking out on her own with Justin. "Fine, but try to keep your mouth shut."

"Mum's the word, dear sister."

"Yeah, right."

Justin plunked himself down on the sofa. Claudia chose the chair, and Zoe plopped down on the floor. They all dipped buttered bread into hot chocolate for a few moments before Claudia got the conversation rolling. Perhaps the chocolate would mellow out the conversation. She could always hope.

"So, Justin, Peter is most likely going to be there at Aunt May's house."

"Yep." He popped another soggy piece of bread in his mouth.

"And I just wanted to know if you had any questions or concerns that you wanted me to address before we got there."

"Nope." Another piece of bread went in.

"Nothing?" She tried to keep the incredulousness out of her voice, but the glare Zoe shot at her told her she had been wrong.

"No, nothing. Can I go now?" No more toast popping this time, but his mouth was set in a line she knew was seconds away from quivering with near tears.

"I'd really like to talk about this with you, Justin. I can't imagine that it's all just as peachy-keen fine as you're trying to make it out to be. Talk to me and we'll sort things out before we get there." Zoe pinched Claudia's calf through her pajama pants, but Claudia ignored her.

"There's nothing to sort out, Mom. I'll be just fine. The guy didn't want me all those years ago, and I don't want him now. So I'm just going to go and see all my real family, and hope Grandpa will give me something cool, and then come home and play some video games." He got up this time without waiting for her to let him go. He didn't precisely stomp back to his room, but it was a close thing.

She was so tempted to go after him, to explain that Peter's desertion had never had anything to do with Justin, but she didn't have any new words to give him, and obviously the ones she'd been saying for years had never penetrated.

Resting her head back against the top of the couch, Claudia released the breath she'd been holding, while letting just one single tear leak from her eye. "Well, I guess that didn't go nearly as bad as it could have gone. Right?" She rolled her head to look at Zoe still sitting on the floor, eating the rest of the toast.

"Sure, Claudia. He could have actually stomped down the hall instead of merely shuffling loudly."

"You're not helping." Closing her eyes, Claudia took a deep breath. "Should I go follow him?"

"Honestly?"

"Yes, honestly. I'm not going to ask you to lie to me."

"Then, no. I think you should let him go. He's probably anxious and nervous right now. You gave him the opportunity to open up to you if he needed to, and he knows you're here for him. I think that's all you can do at this point without making him angry and defensive. If you keep going at him about it, then he's going to think his response is wrong or his feelings are wrong, and that will just make things worse." Zoe rose from the floor, taking the empty toast plate with her.

Claudia took a sip of her rapidly cooling hot

chocolate. Perhaps there was only so much she could do, but that didn't stop her from feeling helpless—and hopeless that today was going to pass by without a serious hiccup in her stride and Justin's.

****

A lazy Sunday morning ranked right up there with some of the finer things in life, as far as Nate was concerned. The buzz of lawnmowers run by more energetic people than himself created a dull hum to punctuate how little Nate planned on doing today. He'd told Claudia he might show at the lunch at May's today, but he was still debating whether that would be a good idea.

Rolling across his big king-sized bed, he grabbed the remote control from the nightstand and flipped on the flat screen he'd hung on the wall opposite the bed. Stacking his hands behind his head, he let the sheet ride low on his hips. This was the life. Quiet mornings with no one else to take care of, no plans but those he made, and no demands on his time that he didn't want.

The news played low across the room. He watched with half his attention because the other half was gnawing on the thought of Claudia and how she had kissed him last night. He had told himself it was a fluke, but he was hard pressed to believe that in the light of day.

What if she did want more? What if his lazy Sunday morning involved lying in bed with a half-dressed Claudia, her hair spread out against his navy-blue pillowcase? Morning snuggling and her giggle under the covers. A knock on the door as they covered up for Justin to come busting through the bedroom door and jump on the bed, demanding Nate come out to play baseball with him in the backyard…

He could almost see it, and that frightened him. He and Claudia enjoyed a comfortable friendship, a way of having each other's backs without smothering. Sharing the little things and the big things. If they did get together, they'd still have all that plus the giggles under the covers, but the potential for disaster was bigger, since it could all be gone in the time it took to utter one or two words that couldn't be taken back in an argument.

Restless now with his thoughts and doubts, Nate climbed out of bed, heading for the shower. The phone rang before he could get there. He thought about leaving it to the answering machine, but since today was the big lunch day, he picked it up. It could be Claudia in need of some last-minute support. He wasn't planning on going to the lunch at May's until it was nearly over, simply because he didn't know how much Peter he could stand in a day. Being available for Claudia was important, though.

As soon as Nate picked up the receiver, Justin started talking in a low voice. "Can you talk, Nate? I have a problem, and I think I need a man-to-man talk."

It was the equivalent of the emergency girl meetings held by Claudia, Zoe, and May, and Nate knew enough to take the call seriously. "What's up, buddy? Are you getting ready for the lunch over at your Aunt May's house?" Glancing at the clock on the nightstand, he realized it was only eight-thirty in the morning, too early for Claudia to start everyone dressing for a lunch.

"Not yet. Even my mom isn't that fanatical about stuff."

Nate laughed at the way Justin almost mirrored Nate's thoughts. "Good word, guy. I guess you are learning some stuff in school."

Normally Justin would have laughed, too, but he didn't this time. It made Nate pull up his joking immediately.

"What's up, guy? Do you need me to come get you for an hour or so? Talk to your mom?" Nate tried to never come between Justin and Claudia, and he certainly did everything he could not to step on her parental toes, but this might be the one time he overrode that unspoken rule.

"Nah, Mom wouldn't take too well to me leaving right now. My grandparents are coming to get me in about thirty minutes to go to church, but I have to talk to you. I'm in my closet with the cordless. Can you talk?"

"Of course, Justin. What do you need?" Nate's shower could definitely wait for this.

There was a long pause on the other end on the line, but Nate waited. Justin was one of those kids who could not be prodded to open up. He had to come out with it in his own time.

"My mom just tried to talk to me about Peter being my biological father."

"How'd that go?" This was a touchy subject no matter how you looked at it or when you tried to address it.

"Not so good. I left the room when she tried to get me to tell her how I felt. I hate all that sappy crappy talk."

Nate didn't call him on the crappy thing since he himself would have said much worse. "Okay. And now you're hiding out in your closet?"

"Well, kind of. I don't want her to say anything else, because she always gets this really sad look in her eyes when she talks about me not having a father. And it bugs the crap out of me because I don't think I missed out on anything, especially because I have you. But I can't tell her that, because then she gets all teary-eyed and says things like 'I'm sorry he left you,' and then it gets worse. I just avoid it altogether, usually, but now that this bozo is here, I can't anymore. And I really, *really* do not want to see him today, but Mom's going to make me. It's going to be a really screwed-up day. You know?"

His words had all come out in a rush, but Nate knew where he was coming from. "Look, Justin, I'm going to be straight with you, okay?"

A brief hesitation and then Justin said, "Okay."

"Your mom does her best job with you. And part of her best job is to make sure that you're loved and to also make sure that if you have to talk to someone you know you can talk to her, even if it's an uncomfortable conversation."

Justin's sigh gusted through the phone. "I know."

"So part of that whole thing involves her bringing up subjects that you might think don't need to be talked about but ones your mom isn't sure how you feel about, right?"

"Yeah."

"Then it follows that she wants you to know you can talk to her about Peter if you want. I know she hasn't always said a lot about him, hardly anyone does, but it doesn't mean he doesn't exist."

"I wish he didn't."

"But if he didn't, then you wouldn't, and that would take a certain midget light out of *my* life." A laugh from Justin followed that felt like a pot of gold at the end of this thorny rainbow.

"Yeah, who would you have to trounce you at basketball if I wasn't around?"

"No one, and that would be so sad for my ego." Nate smiled and sat on the end of his bed. "Look, my best advice is to go in there today and show Peter what a good guy you are and what a great job your mom has done raising you. You don't have to interact with him any more than you want to, but I know your Aunt May is anxious for you to meet Peter, since this is the first time he's come home after you were born. But you have every right to treat him like a stranger. You don't have to call him Dad or give him a hug or anything. You just go in, say hi, tell him you love your mom, and then walk out with your head up. He's the one who lacks something, not you. He's the one who missed out, not you, and certainly not your mom. You're a great guy, and he'll know that right away. Got it?"

"You're the best, Nate. Thanks for not getting all girly-gushy on me."

"That's what guys are for, Justin. Hang in there. Give your mom a break in all this, and have a good time. I can't wait to see what Roger thinks you want from his possessions. Maybe he'll give you one of those dead stuffed animal heads on the wall of his study."

Justin pretended to gag, and they chatted for a few more moments before Justin said his grandparents were there to pick him up and his mom was banging on the door. Nate set the phone down on the nightstand and stood massaging the back of his neck for a moment. He hoped he had done the right thing. It felt like the right thing, so it couldn't be all bad.

Grabbing his towel, he moved toward the shower again. And the phone rang, again. He really needed to think about installing Caller ID. Who else was calling him on a Sunday morning?

"Hello?"

"Hey, Nate, my boyo," his grandmother said in far too frail a voice. "You need to come over here and help your granny. I think I'm not in too good a shape, and your mom's out doing some grocery shopping while all those churchgoers are pretending to do more than preen in their fancy clothes. Might be a heart attack or something. If you could hurry?"

Nate was already out the door and in his car with the cordless still against his ear. "I'll be right there." He floored it, not caring that he only wore sleeping pants and yesterday's T-shirt.

Throwing the phone on the seat, he made a beeline for his mom's house and whatever happened to be waiting for him there. It looked like he might not be able to make the lunch today, but he was sure Claudia and Justin would do just fine without him tagging along to run interference that they wouldn't need. They were strong and had each other. They always had.

****

"For the last time, Zoe, I'm fine!" Claudia enunciated each word clearly and slowly, as if explaining a particularly difficult concept to a small child. They had an hour left until the lunch at May's, and Zoe had not let up, even for a second, since Claudia had tromped into her room hoping to escape Zoe's presence and unwanted fashion consult on Claudia's closet.

Slamming the armoire door closed, Claudia whipped around, blonde hair flying in her face, to stare her sister down. She knew she sounded bitchy, but she didn't care anymore. This day could just go right to hell. She'd gladly provide the handbasket.

She understood that Zoe wanted her to look good for this meeting, to "wow" Peter, in Zoe's words. But after her initial thoughts of panic and making him miss what he'd thrown away, she no longer wanted to deal with that kind of crap. She just wanted to survive it. He would be gone soon, and she wouldn't be a thought in his head—the same as it had been for ten years. Dressing the part of some vixen was not going to change that. In fact, she didn't want it to. Part of her almost wanted to dress dowdy so as not to draw attention to herself. Pull out another pair of flats and fade into the wallpaper. Though that went against everything female inside her, it was still tempting. Not that Zoe the Harpy would let her.

In the end, she'd decided she was actually going to pull a Peter—get in, get what she wanted, and get the hell out before the fireworks started.

Zoe flopped onto her back on Claudia's satin bedspread and heaved an exaggerated sigh as she lifted her sandal-clad feet into the air and pointed her painted toes toward the ceiling. "All I'm saying is that you should at least think about wearing something sexy. It would be good for your ego, especially now. You can go, devastate him wearing one of your new fabulous dresses, and leave him breathing hard."

"This from the woman who won't even give a certain lawyer a chance? I find it hard to believe you feel that way." Claudia stuck her tongue out, but then immediately turned serious. "And it's not that simple. Sure, the awe at my current beauty would be great, but what if Peter tries to talk to me? What do I do then? 'Hi, Peter, how are you? It's been a long time. Oh, by the way, your son is growing like a weed and becoming a wonderful person along the way, but I guess that wasn't important enough for even a phone call in the last ten years? Your whole family was able to connect with this great kid in some way, but not you.' That would go over really well." Her voice almost dripped with sarcasm. She took great satisfaction in slamming hangers back and forth in her closet, looking for something to wear that said, "I did fine without you, now go home!"

Zoe had been only fifteen when Peter left Claudia pregnant, but she was one of the few people Claudia had confided in when she was scared, terrified of giving birth and doing it alone. Of all people, Claudia thought her sister understood. She'd been there when Claudia had peed on the first pregnancy indicator—and the second, and the third. She'd gone with Claudia to all her doctor's appointments. She'd held Claudia's hand when Claudia had told their parents that she was going to have a baby. Why was she pushing so hard, knowing so much about how this was not some lark?

For her part, Zoe wasn't without sympathy. "I'll tell you what, Claude. I'll walk in first and do reconnaissance. I'll keep him distracted and won't let him talk to you at all. But I still think you should wear the sexy outfit, or at least one that shows off a little cleavage. And your hair has to be perfect. He needs to pay at least a little for walking out." Zoe stopped and stared at her feet as she rotated her ankles clockwise—her only brush with exercise.

"I'm not interested in him paying for anything." But in her head she couldn't deny the little spark of something that said it wouldn't be a bad thing to look great when she had to face Peter again. She'd ignore him, but if he couldn't ignore her… Well, maybe that wouldn't be so bad.

She shooed Zoe out and got down to the business of looking fabulous. She ignored the ringing phone, trusting Zoe to get it while she pulled out her brushes, compacts, lipstick, and eyeliner.

"Are you ready?" Zoe called through the door twenty minutes later. Thankfully, May had chosen the day the shop was closed to have this lunch, since everyone was involved, but Zoe was driving her crazy with being a time cop.

Claudia thunked her head against her dressing table. This was such an incredibly, horribly bad idea. What had she been thinking? She couldn't sit in the same room with Peter without a care in the world. She had been thinking exactly nothing. She shouldn't be going at all.

"Come on, Claude. We need to leave right now if we're going to get to May's on time." She banged on the door this time, probably to emphasize her point.

Not that Claudia needed any kind of emphasis. Her stomach was already heaving with rabid squirrels.

More knocking.

"Damn it, Zoe, I'm coming." Shoving herself up from the padded vanity chair, she took one last minute to check her hair and her makeup. She looked fine. She wasn't going to worry about it anymore. Either she was ready or she wasn't. It was as simple as that.

And beyond that, she wasn't the one who had left. He was, so he should be the one worrying about how he looked and what his reception would be like.

"Come on, Claudia, put a rush on it. We need to go!"

More banging, and Claudia wanted to bang her head against the wall. "I'm coming. Hold your freaking horses." She satisfied her need to bang by slamming her bedroom door open and stalking down the hall. "You wanted me to take the time to look fabulous, and now all of a sudden you're trying to rush me out of the house. What gives? Mom and Dad aren't picking up Justin from church for another half an hour, and lunch doesn't even start until at least one. What's the rush?"

Zoe flicked her hair over her shoulder and looked over Claudia's shoulder at the wedding picture that had hung on the wall since their mother and father had originally lived here twenty years ago.

"Zoe, I'm over here." Claudia snapped her fingers.

"Yep. Ready to go?"

Claudia planted herself in front of her sister. "No, I'm ready to hear what's going on that you won't look at me."

The phone chose that moment to ring.

"Okay, let's get a move on. We don't want to be late for the lunch. That would be horribly rude, wouldn't it? To be late? So, we should go. Right now. Right. Now." Zoe pushed and prodded, but Claudia leaned back against her as best she could in her three-inch heels.

The answering machine kicked on a second before Claudia snatched the cordless phone off the end table.

She stood with the phone in her hand while their message played. Then she cut her eyes over to Zoe when a man started talking.

"Zoe? Did we have a bad connection or another malfunction? I'm waiting for your answer regarding dinner. You have my card, please call back. And let your business partners know all the paperwork will be ready in a few weeks. Perhaps we could have that champagne toast to celebrate. I'll look forward to hearing from you and hopefully seeing you again soon."

The machine beeped and the message light flickered. Claudia took her time turning toward Zoe. She placed a hand on her hip and used the other hand to point the phone at her sister. "And who might that be?"

"That might be Grandma." Zoe shrugged and continued to avoid all eye contact.

"Try again. Grandma didn't start taking testosterone in the last three days since I talked to her."

"That might be Justin's principal calling to see if you want a parent-teacher meeting."

"Didn't sound like it to me." Claudia dropped the phone on the couch.

Zoe heaved a sigh. "That might be our lawyer, who won't take no for an answer."

"And why would our lawyer be calling you about champagne celebrations?"

"We really should get going." Zoe headed out the door with Claudia close on her heels.

"But I want to talk about Mr. Zegray," Claudia said in a sing-song voice as they walked down the outside staircase. "Or is it Dexter? The Dex-Man. Is he ambi-Dex-trous?"

Color shot into Zoe's face. "It's Dex." She opened the car door and practically threw herself into the driver's seat.

"Ooh, Dex. And is Dex a total paper-bag wearer? Is he a doggie? Was he thwacked by the ugly stick? Need extra deodorant? A candidate for the Darwin Award? I thought he made you hot to trot."

Cranking the key too hard, Zoe whipped around and faced Claudia. "No, all right? No, he's not a doggie. He's actually extremely cute and pretty damn sexy, too. But he's a total Dog with a capital D."

"Oh, sorry." Claudia clipped her seatbelt and smoothed her dress over her thighs. She let the silence hang in the air for a few blocks while Zoe drove with her eyes straight forward. "So, really cute?"

Zoe sighed, and her shoulders slumped. "Extremely cute."

"Irrefutable proof he's a capital-D Dog?"

Another sigh. "I don't know how else you can explain five bouquets to five different women in as many weeks."

"Oh." Yeah, that didn't look good, and even though Claudia might want her sister to get out and actually find someone who would make her heart sing, she also didn't want her to get crushed before she even made it out the door. A womanizer was a sure way to get stomped.

"Yeah, sucks." Zoe made the left onto May's street.

"But Uncle Al likes him."

"Just because he could be a good lawyer doesn't necessarily mean he's a good human being."

And didn't that just about sum it up? Peter had

been a good person but a miserable father-to-be for the few months he'd stuck around. Nate was oblivious and was a good friend, but there was no guarantee he'd be a better lover than a friend. Why couldn't things be simpler? And this was a funny time to be asking that question, since she was about to walk into the figurative lion's den and come head to head with Peter for the first time in a long time.

****

It was a letdown to get all the way to May's and have Peter out and about somewhere. Claudia had wanted to walk in, face him down, and then have that over with. Instead she would have to wait. She was not very good at waiting.

May came into the kitchen where Claudia was taking a breather for a moment in anticipation of Peter coming back. She had been trying to think where she should be when he arrived so as not to be caught off guard or in a position of less power. The kitchen was her only option at this point. The familiar environment was calming to her nerves. And if things got too bad, she could always whip up a cake to burn off some of her nervous energy.

May came breezing in with a smile on her perpetually happy face. Why couldn't Claudia have that?

"So what are the plans for the addition to Decadence like, Claude?" May asked, opening the freezer to fill up the ice bucket again.

"Oh, I, um, didn't understand them."

Turning around, May pierced her with a look. "Nate didn't explain them to you?"

"Well, he didn't stay around long enough for us to

get into that." That was an understatement.

"What did he stay around long enough to get into?" May's chuckle was knowing, but it made a hard ball of regret sink into Claudia's stomach.

"Nothing."

The smile turned down a bit as May stared at her. "Emergency girl meeting?"

"Nah, it'll be fine." As soon as she got over feeling like a complete nitwit, at least.

"And you're being cryptic."

She was, but she did not want to broach this subject when Peter could walk in at any moment. That would be beyond awkward. She changed the subject. "How is it, having Peter back home?"

"It's nice, I guess." May wouldn't look Claudia in the eyes. "He hasn't been back here in over ten years, and it's nice to see him in the house again. I feel so divided over everything, though." Her gaze flicked up to Claudia, then back down quickly to the ice bucket in her hands. "He *is* my brother, and we hung out for years before we even met you and Zoe. I don't know." She went at the stubborn ice cubes from the bucket with a little too much force, in Claudia's opinion. "He's out right now picking up some last-minute things for me. He should be here any moment, actually." She turned to get more ice. When she turned back, her expression was no longer dreamy, but sad. "I just wish he'd had more to do with Justin all these years, so this didn't have to be so awkward for everyone."

"More to do with him?" Claudia tried hard to keep the sarcasm out of her voice. "Don't you mean anything?"

May stiffened. "This is a subject we're not going to

be able to agree on, so let's drop it. I'm angry with him, too, but he's still my family."

Claudia felt like a heel. "No, you're right. I'm sorry. I shouldn't have said anything. I'm just on edge. I don't want to fight with you."

May moved in for a hug. "I don't want to fight, either. I don't want to be on the outs with you."

Claudia let herself be held and then stepped back. "We'll get through this fine. I've done well for myself over the years, and I'm not pining after him, so I bet it won't even be a problem. Plus, it has been over ten years, like you said. I doubt we'll even really come in contact with each other while he's here for the week."

"Yeah. How is Zoe doing with everything? Do you think she'll be on her best behavior?" May picked up a tray of relish and set it back down. She put the paper towels in the refrigerator and the butter in the sink.

"Zoe promised to be good. I guess we'll have to take her at her word. But I might not be here very long. I'm going to do my best, though, to hang tough." Claudia watched May for another few moments while she moved the salt and pepper shakers to the window sill. "Something wrong?"

"Ah, no. Why?"

Claudia pulled the paper towels out of the refrigerator, put the salt and pepper on the table, and placed the butter back on the counter. "You seem distracted all of a sudden. Are you sure nothing's wrong?"

May shook her head and laughed. "I'm positive. I'm just a little out of sorts." She dusted her hands off on a kitchen towel, then grabbed the tray of relish again. "Let's get everything out on the table. I'm sure the guys are hungry."

"Don't we want to wait for everyone else to get here? I haven't seen Mom and Dad yet, and they're bringing Justin." Which would be a set of fireworks all on its own. "They'll be here soon. I'm sure Brad's fine with entertaining Zoe for a bit. No one else needs anything."

"Zoe doesn't need entertaining," Zoe said, appearing in the kitchen doorway to the living room. "She does, however, want to finally corner Claudia to talk about what happened with Nate yesterday afternoon. Since you've avoided me for the last twenty-four hours, I thought I'd wrangle May into helping me get you to spill what happened."

Claudia opened her mouth to respond and nothing came out but a squeak. "I don't know what happened." Claudia felt her cheeks grow bright red and knew she was doomed. Here came the interrogation. With Peter most likely on his way here, she did not want to have this conversation right here and right now.

"Interesting. Very interesting," Zoe said. "What's the blush for?"

"Nothing." Claudia washed her hands at the sink, then turned around to ask May what else there was to do, completely ignoring Zoe's question.

"It's all finished," May said with a smug smile. "But you're not doing anything but explaining that flush to your face." May threw a dish towel over her shoulder, then leaned back against the counter.

"Nothing's going on." Claudia washed her hands again and kept her back to them.

May's hand landed on Claudia's left shoulder just as Zoe's landed on her right.

"You can't hide from us." And Zoe wasn't going to let her.

May must have had the same idea. "We're not leaving this kitchen until you tell us what's happening."

This ought to be interesting and could definitely be tough. Claudia had spent a lot of time building up walls, and sometimes she could outlast the most avid askers. That didn't always hold true when dealing with her two best girl friends, though.

"I was just talking to Nate to see how his day was going." That was certainly true to some extent.

"And that made you blush—why? You've talked to Nate about the very same thing every day for years." May seemed to be enjoying herself way too much with this. Claudia wracked her brain to come up with a way to get them onto a different topic, but nothing was coming to her.

"But maybe she finally screwed up her courage to do more than bat her eyelashes at him." Zoe squinted at Claudia, then laughed. "Oh, yeah, looks like I may have hit the nail on the head."

"What is this? Where was I?" May looked back and forth between Claudia and Zoe.

"It was nothing," Claudia said.

"Nothing?" Zoe said loudly enough for Claudia to hush her. "That's not what you said after Nate left without going over the plans with you." She turned to May. "You should have seen her face and the way her lips were all rosy when Justin and I came back from picking up some hoagies. She said she'd explain to me what happened but then magically was not available after that. She even took an hour-long shower last night to avoid me."

"I was not exactly avoiding you."

"Oh, yes, you were! And you're trying to get out of talking about it now."

Claudia blew out an exasperated sigh. Apparently, they would be doing this here and now instead of waiting. If Peter walked in, she'd just do what damage control she could. Or she would just not care, since he had nothing to do with her anymore. That was the better option.

Zoe shuffled around the kitchen, rearranging all the other things May had put into the wrong places, while Claudia explained the kiss in the kitchen and May squealed.

"Well, the only problem is that he's acting like nothing happened. I'm confused, but I'm still going for it. He's not going to ignore me this time." Her resolve was firm, just as long as his wasn't as firmly set to keep his distance from her.

"Absolutely! So are you going to take him out on a date?" Zoe asked. "I can stay home and hang out with Justin."

The kitchen door swung open and all conversation stopped when Peter walked onto May's red-and-white-checked linoleum. He stared at the three of them, and they stared back. Claudia held her breath. Zoe had a tendency to blurt the first thing that came to mind. While it would probably serve him right, it would be terribly unflattering and would probably upset May more than she already was. Not worth it, especially since it would not be conducive to getting through this with her dignity intact.

Claudia wanted to see if Zoe was fuming but found herself locked in a stare-down with Peter, a faint smile on her face. Should she be plotting revenge, or reliving old memories? Taking comfort in what could be with Nate, or wondering what could have been with Peter?

Even that thought was cut off when Justin, followed by her parents, stepped through the door right behind Peter.

****

Peter Drake heard the commotion behind him but couldn't take his eyes off Claudia Bradley. She was stunning in a soft-looking, short-sleeved black dress that stopped mid thigh and flirted with her enhanced curves. He stood transfixed, seeing the girl he'd fumbled around with in the back seat of his Mustang had morphed into this exquisite woman. She still had the clearest gray eyes he'd ever seen.

Time seemed to stop, and the very air grew still in his sister's kitchen. So many images skittered across his mind. Laughing with Claudia, tugging on her long braid to tip her head back so he could kiss her, the way the backs of her hands were always so soft when she'd brush them against his cheek.

But then a childish voice said, "Excuse me, sir," walking past him.

The connection between him and Claudia broke. He looked down to see the child and stared into his own brown eyes. His first urge was to ruffle the dark hair a couple shades lighter than his own. He noticed the missing eyetooth and felt his own adult eyetooth with his tongue.

The sound of someone clearing her throat jerked his gaze up to the woman standing to the boy's right. Claudia's mother shook her head and let a small frown take over her face.

He got her message, though it had been a long time since she'd looked at him. Since she'd done any kind of communication with him, silent or otherwise. He'd always been her favorite, and he was surprised she'd even look at him at this point.

"Mona," he said, trying to still the quiver in his voice. He'd never allowed himself to even look at the pictures May sent him or the ones she carried in her wallet and tried to shove in his face. It wasn't in his nature to look back once he'd made a decision. He'd stuck with that all these years, but now he feared he might not be able to walk away unscathed or unaffected by this afternoon. Damn May and his father for making this unavoidable.

"It's a surprise to see you here...Sparky." Mona placed a protective arm around the boy's shoulders and pulled him into her side.

Somehow she made his old nickname sound like "jackass," but he probably deserved no less. And he was very aware she hadn't called him by name. Now wasn't the time to introduce himself to his son, not in the middle of the kitchen, with his hands full of grocery bags.

"It's a surprise to be here, Mrs. Bradley. I...um...should hand these things to..." He couldn't think of his sister's name. Ah-ha! "May. I should give these things to May." With jerky movements, he handed the bags to May and was careful to avoid Claudia's eyes. There was so much tension in the tiny kitchen it felt like it was going to explode. Should he excuse himself? Did the boy know who he was? Care who he was? He would keep things vague. He didn't know what the boy had been told, but he didn't want to make waves. This

117

was the first time he was face to face with him, but he didn't want to make any promises he couldn't keep.

And since he'd given away his rights all those years ago, he didn't want to anger Claudia now by trying to slip in under her radar. In fact, he doubted Mrs. Bradley would let him.

What exactly had he given up all those years ago? And would he ever be able to get the boy's face out of his head? Did he want to? Did he deserve to? The child looked healthy. Peter continued to stare at the miniature version of himself, so similar to how he'd looked almost twenty years ago.

When he first pulled into the driveway at his sister's house, he'd remained in the car for a moment and rested his head on the steering wheel. He didn't want to go in and face Claudia, much less the boy. He couldn't even bring himself to call the boy his son. Because he wasn't.

Peter may have donated the sperm, but he'd never been a father. How could he face the woman he'd professed to love and then left?

He'd grabbed the bags in the back seat and exited the car. He would face her the same way he'd faced business associates through the years. He wasn't a coward. At least he wasn't anymore.

And if she wouldn't even look at him, he'd deal with it. He'd bluff his way through. But now that he was faced with both Claudia and the boy, he didn't think bluffing was going to do him any good.

"You can put the stuff away." May gave him back the bags.

Everyone else left the room en masse, no one speaking except for the boy's chattering. He had never felt more alone in a crowd.

"Make sure you stash the cheese and whatever else you got into the refrigerator. Oh, and thanks for picking everything up," May said as he continued to stand there, the bags dangling from his hands. "I have this one last tray to set out, and then we're ready to eat."

"Okay."

Something about his one-word response must have hit her wrong, because she put the tray down and really looked at him. She grabbed his chin and turned his head from side to side. "I know that was hard, and I wish there had been more preparation. Are you going to be all right? Did anything happen while you were out?"

"I simply went to the grocery store, May. I'll be fine." He ducked behind the refrigerator door, not wanting her to be able to see his face. He'd stay in here forever if he could, to avoid looking her in the eyes right now. He'd been in front of a woman and baby in the grocery store line earlier. He'd made it through the line with his purchases and paid from his wallet, where there weren't any pictures of the child he'd helped create. The woman behind him was gushing about her newborn and had nearly an accordion file of those plastic inserts to hold wallet-sized photos, all of them filled.

"Isn't he the cutest thing?" she'd said. "I mean, the birth was hard and all, but to hold him in my arms, to snuggle him—it's the best feeling in the whole wide world."

He'd gathered his two plastic bags as she pulled an envelope out of her bag and removed more pictures, putting them on the little panel normally used for signing credit card receipts. The cashier cooed over each new image, and Peter walked out of the grocery store with their words ringing in his ears. The encounter had haunted him the whole way back to the house.

"You can talk to me, you know," May said now, tugging on the back of his belt.

"It was nothing."

"It wasn't 'nothing' if you won't even look at me. It's also not 'nothing' if you're not telling me to stop pulling on your fancy dress pants because it will ruin the perfect crease."

She had him there, but now wasn't the time to bring all this churning up. "Can we talk about it later?" It would at least appease her until he could figure out how to broach a subject he had never let her talk about to him.

"Look at me first."

"I'm trying to put the groceries away. Don't you have guests to see to?"

But apparently she wasn't falling for it. He hadn't heard her leaving the room, and he felt silly with his head all but buried in the cake sitting on the top shelf. Backing out, he turned slowly to face his sister, someone he'd shared all his secrets with until he'd started dating Claudia.

"Do you promise to talk later?" She folded her hands at her stomach and gave him an unblinking stare.

"Yes, I promise. I will speak with you about it later. After everyone has gone." Especially Claudia. God, how was he going to face her at the table? And the child would probably sit right next to her. Should he try to pull her aside and find out what the boy knew before they sat down? Maybe Peter would simply stay in the kitchen all afternoon.

But there was May, tugging him into the next room with one hand while her other balanced the tray of lettuce, tomato, onions, and pickles. He came along willingly, not wanting to ruin the food. He could handle this. He was a professional. He'd been through uncomfortable meetings before. He could suck it up, be in an awkward position, without a single person knowing for sure that he wasn't fine.

This would be no different. Except it was, as soon as he cleared the door, came into the dining room where everyone congregated, and saw Claudia again. She looked exactly as she had in high school, full of vibrancy and life. A spark of light in a room crowded with shadows.

Her sister Zoe raised an eyebrow to him when she saw his gaze stay on Claudia. She shook her head at him, and almost looked smug. But a part of him broke off and dissipated, knowing Claudia was here but would most likely avoid him for the whole time.

And if she didn't have a ring on and was here by herself, did it mean she was still available? He hadn't heard that she'd married or was dating anyone seriously. But then again, he hadn't asked. He didn't think May would have kept that kind of information to herself, though.

He didn't have time to dwell on that horrible path for long, since Brad came up and clapped him on the shoulder and began talking stocks and bonds. This conversation he could understand and participate in. The one scheduled with May later this evening had the spit drying up in his mouth.

****

"Are you going to be okay?" Zoe slipped a hand

into Claudia's and squeezed as they sat on the couch in May's living room.

Taking stock, Claudia nodded. Sure, she'd put on thirty pounds since high school. Originally she'd called it the baby fat left over from her pregnancy, but she highly doubted she could still claim the same thing after ten years. Her fat was as old as her son. Jeez, that was nothing if not severely depressing.

But she'd be fine. There was something almost surreal about being in the same room with Peter after so long, but she'd survive. "I'm fine. I should probably go say hello to him so we don't have to circle each other all afternoon."

"I think that's a bad idea. He should have to come to you."

"Yeah, well, that's what you think. And since I'm the one who has to live with it, I think I should go with my gut instinct." She set her cup on an end table and straightened her skirt, watching Brad and Peter talking near the other couch across the room. May's dad sat in an easy chair, drifting between sleep and wakefulness.

It would be easier to do this on her own terms and surrounded by the people of her choosing rather than be caught off guard. And she still smarted from the conversation she'd tried to have with Justin earlier.

Surprisingly, Justin hadn't yet come in from the game room in the basement to ask where he was. In fact, her son hadn't even responded to Peter in the kitchen, other than to say, "Excuse me." At least he'd used his manners, which wasn't always a sure thing, and hadn't embarrassed her into thinking she'd raised a hooligan.

Before she could lose her courage, she lifted her

chin and walked across the room, trying not to think about how she felt more like she was waddling. She hadn't been a skinny thing at seventeen, and at twenty-eight she certainly wasn't. She sensed Zoe close on her heels but ignored her. It would be hard enough to do this without clinging to her younger, hostile sister.

The small expanse of carpet in May's living room had never seemed bigger. It was like one of those nightmares where you can't seem to get to the end of the hall because it continues to stretch out in front of you. But finally she did make it over to Peter. His back was turned to her, and she studied the hairline at the back of his neck. It looked freshly shaven, with a thin strip of white skin under the close-cut hair. She used to trace her fingers just there when they sat at football games and froze in the winter. It was always exposed by his knit caps. She wasn't sure what it meant that she felt nothing at the memory but a brief surge of nostalgia.

She shook her head slightly to clear it of the image that wouldn't do any good in helping her get through the next several minutes. At least there wasn't an inch-wide strip of naked skull where the hair plugs had not been put in right. Although it might have been easier to do this if Peter had turned into a frumpy, pudgy old man in the last ten years.

She tried to steel herself against looking into Peter's face and seeing her son in twenty or so years. From pictures of Peter as a boy, she knew Justin looked very like his father at this age. If nothing else, at least she knew her boy was going to be good-looking when he was older.

And she'd stalled long enough. "Hello, Peter."

Chapter Six

After what felt like an eternity, Peter finally turned around. She hadn't spent the time to look anywhere else than at his eyes, in the kitchen. And that had felt more like a tractor beam she couldn't disengage from than anything she actually wanted to be a part of. Claudia hadn't seen any pictures of him in years. May knew better than to bring them out. Or bring him up, for that matter. He was the tabooest of subjects.

So she still had a picture of him in her head as an eighteen-year-old with bronzed skin, dark hair, and perfect smile that could turn her knees to jelly across the cafeteria table.

And there wasn't much different about him now. He'd filled out a little, had more of a man's body, but the smile was still there, the bronzed skin was still kissed by the sun, and the dark hair didn't contain a single strand of gray. Thank God she'd gotten her hair dyed last week and her knees were rock solid.

"Claudia."

And his voice was still as sinful as ever. It slid over her skin and down her throat. Damn it. Nate. She'd think about Nate and forget the smile. But she couldn't even pull up a decent picture of Nate in her mind now. She was surprised she'd remembered his name. Her knees would not turn to jelly now if they knew what was good for them. Finally an image popped into her mind, the one with Nate and his shirt halfway up that scrumptious belly the other day. The forced smile on her face relaxed a half inch.

And then they did the awkward dance—Do you give a hug? Kiss the air next to his cheek? Shake hands? Keep ten feet between you? God, this was killing her.

She settled on a hybrid—the one-armed hug. But Peter was attempting the very same thing and ended up getting a handful of her boob.

She jumped back faster than she thought she could possibly move and blushed to the roots of her hair.

He, on the other hand, smirked and looked just like the old Peter, sure he could get everything in the world handed to him on the platter without any work or investment in anything other than himself.

"Well, it was nice seeing you." She started to walk away and realized she couldn't go any farther than the kitchen. The joke was on her. She couldn't duck out of lunch before lunch even happened, couldn't leave May in the lurch. So she'd have to buck it up.

"Zoe, could I see you in the kitchen?" If she had to be in the house, she'd make sure it wasn't right near him. Certainly something must need to be done before they all sat down at the table and acted like one big happy family.

"Right behind you."

Taking careful steps back across the living room, which seemed to have grown even larger, she heard May talking in a low voice to Peter and then a solid thwack when she smacked him in the back of the head. Claudia barely contained a snicker and wondered when the hell her life had become this insane weirdness.

"Well, that went well, don't you think?" Zoe yanked open the refrigerator, dove inside and came up triumphant. She tore into a crisp carrot like she was taking off someone's head.

"Yeah, that wasn't uncomfortable at all. And you were a real big help. Thanks." Claudia searched without any luck for something, anything, to do. "You could have at least said hello."

After slamming the refrigerator door with more force than necessary, Zoe gave Claudia a hard look with glittering eyes. "If you really thought I was going to say hi to that man and give him a hug, you are completely off your rocker. I barely could promise May I'd be civil. Hugs were so not on the list."

Claudia couldn't help it. All the tension, all the stress, all the anticipation of the first time she talked to Peter again after so many years came bubbling out in near-hysterical laughter. She gripped the counter as the sound came rolling out in waves. She accepted the paper towel Zoe gave her and mopped at her eyes, no longer sure if she was laughing or crying.

For her part, Zoe came over and wrapped an arm around Claudia's shoulders. "I know it was hard for you, but I think you did a wonderful job and had a lot of class. You knocked him for a loop."

"I'll say." May's voice made Claudia jump back from the comfort of Zoe's arms.

Feeling guilty when she shouldn't, Claudia wrung her hands in front of her. "I...um...just thought there might be something I could do to get things ready for the lunch. Thought I'd come check out the kitchen and see what I could do to help." But when Claudia looked around the spotless kitchen with its blindingly white appliances and fancy café curtains done in red and white, she knew there was nothing here for her but shelter.

"You'll say what?" Zoe's chin took on the belligerent set she used to wear when their mother told her curfew was at ten, no exceptions.

May took her time staring at the two of them, and Claudia saw the storm brewing in her eyes. This could go from bad to worse in two seconds flat if she didn't step in and play peacekeeper. "Hi, May, thanks for not making that awkward."

Obviously it was the wrong thing to say, because May's normally warm brown eyes took on the temperature of rock-hard chocolate ice cream. "I didn't have to make it awkward. But I think someone else was doing a damn fine job of turning that around." She threw a stack of napkins onto the big butcher block island and stomped around the kitchen to the refrigerator. She yanked it open, much like Zoe had, and attacked another poor carrot, again much like Zoe. Two years younger than Claudia and one older than Zoe, May had always been the bridge over the gap in the sisters' ages when they were younger. This had to be hard for her, too.

"I'm sorry, May. I didn't mean to sound flippant. I didn't know what it was going to be like to be in the same room as Peter again after all this time. I was simply saying that I was glad it didn't involve yelling or crying. That's all."

"I'm sure it would have been different if left up to this one." She hooked a thumb at Zoe and decapitated the poor carrot with her teeth.

Zoe visibly bristled. Claudia could almost see the

hair standing up on the back of her neck like some cat being confronted by a dog. Not that Claudia would share that image with anyone outside her own mind. It didn't flatter either one of them.

"Down, Zoe. I can handle this myself." Claudia walked around to the other side of the island and gently took the carrot out of May's hand. She didn't want this to escalate to a point where none of them could be comfortable around each other. Especially since they all worked together. They'd had their tiffs before, but nothing like the potential this had to become an all-out war.

She walked May over to where Zoe stood rigid and made them face her, next to each other. "I'm going to say this once, and then I don't think I ever want to say it again. I want both of you to know that I love you. And I love my son. And I love our store and the beautiful work we do together. Up until this point, we haven't ever discussed Peter or even let him into a conversation peripherally because I think we all knew what a disaster it could be."

"But..."

Claudia held up a hand to stop whatever Zoe was about to say. She held Zoe's right hand and May's left. "Peter gave me something precious. It might not have ever worked out between us. We may have hated each other if he'd stayed around long enough to see Justin take his first steps. But that doesn't negate the fact that we were a couple and we were both in the car the night Justin was conceived."

"He's only back for a few weeks." May squeezed her hand.

"I understand that, May, and I know you want this

visit to go nicely so he'll come back again, but you can't discount the fact that he hasn't even tried to see Justin since he was born, and that he left me to fend for myself almost from the moment the stick turned blue."

"I never have." May tried to pull her hand away, but Claudia wouldn't let her.

"I'm not saying you have, but it's a fact. I made out for myself just fine, but it might not be all roses and icing while he's here. I don't want it to rip us apart, that's all I'm saying."

"It's not going to rip us apart. How could you think that?"

"We're already having problems, right now, and we're barely ten minutes into this occasion. You don't think that's a big deal?" May's attitude baffled Claudia. She had been there in the delivery room. Maybe she hadn't seen all the tears that had fallen in the dark of her room like Zoe had. And she had missed two years of cranky toddler Justin while she went to design school. But that didn't mean she didn't know how hard this was for her.

"We could just avoid the subject while he's here," Zoe said, shrugging.

Claudia was ready to say that was an option, just to keep the status quo, when May cut in.

"No, I think it would be better if we brought it out into the open." She seemed to pluck up her courage and looked first Claudia in the eyes and then Zoe. "Girls' night at your apartment tonight, and we'll sort it out. In the meantime, you did a great job out there, and as far as I know, Peter has no intention of doing anything but staying for a few weeks, at the most. I don't even know if he had plans to see Justin while he was here."

129

Something about that seemed to strike her wrong, but she shook it off, saying, "We'll talk about it later, but if you could just hang out in the same room with him without anything going wrong right now, I'd really appreciate it. I know I already pulled the friendship card to get you here. I don't think I have another one to throw on the table."

"Babe, you don't need to throw another card on the table," Claudia said, hooking an arm over May's shoulder. "This is awkward and difficult for all of us, for different reasons. But we'll get through it." She let go to grab a handful of plastic silverware. "We'll enjoy lunch and figure it all out later. It's not a problem and not nearly as tough as I thought it would be. I can handle it. Don't I always?"

So they went out into the dining room, where everyone had gathered at the buffet on the long oak table Nate had made for May when she and Brad married three years ago. Just the reminder of him and her failed attempts at seducing him made her feel better, for some reason. She was moving on. She was moving forward with something she wanted, and no one, not even the reemergence of an old lover and the father of her child, was going to make her forget that she did have purpose and she did have goals that didn't include him.

Lunch got underway. Justin was called up from the basement and sat next to her in the living room. Since May had so many people there, with her parents and Claudia's parents, her, Justin, and Zoe, everyone pretty much just spread out through the main floor of the house. Thankfully, she didn't see Peter at all. But she was still waiting for Justin to start asking where he was.

She'd finally screwed up her courage just this morning to tell her boy that Peter would be there. At first she'd thought he would be full of questions after he'd walked away the first time, but he'd surprised her by coming back to the living room and talking about the batting cages and some homework that still needed to be done tonight. Then her parents had shown up, and that had been the end of that.

She wasn't going to bring it up while they ate, with Zoe sitting on the living room floor in front of them like a guard dog, but she also knew it would come at some point. She'd be happy if only they could get through this. However, she wasn't holding her breath.

Sure enough, the other shoe dropped just as she put a particularly sour pickle between her lips.

"So, Mom, that guy in there, he was my sperm donor, huh?" Justin shoved some chips in his mouth and settled back into the couch.

He sounded so nonchalant, she almost choked on the pickle. That wouldn't be a very nice picture, so she made an effort to finish chewing and swallow. She shot a look at Zoe. There was only one person who called Peter a sperm donor out loud, and she was staring at her.

Zoe did everything but whistle and rock back and forth on her heels in a picture of total innocence.

Claudia cleared her throat. "Let's not use that term, okay?"

"You mean 'sperm donor'?" he asked loudly. Loudly enough to have several heads in the next room turn to see what was going on.

Claudia inanely laughed and shook her head as if to say "Kids! What are you going to do?" but inside she was ready to throttle him. "Yes, that is the word I'm talking about, and I don't want to hear it again."

"Aunt Zoe says it."

Claudia mentally rolled her eyes and set her foot down on the edge of Zoe's pants when she tried to get up and walk out. "You are not going anywhere."

Zoe at least had the grace to look sheepish. "Yes, ma'am."

Claudia focused all her attention on Justin again and formed the words in her head to make him understand. "We won't call him that because it could hurt his feelings." Now it was Zoe's turn to roll her eyes. Claudia saw it peripherally and let it pass. She didn't know why she was worrying about Peter's feelings either, but it was built into who she was. What happened was in the past, and she wasn't going to drag it all up and examine it because of one lousy lunch.

"So what should I call him?" Justin popped another chip into his mouth, but this time it was feigned nonchalance.

She could almost feel him vibrating next to her. She'd tried over the years to understand what it must feel like to have one of the two people who should love you absolutely without reserve walk out, but all she could do was follow Justin's lead. Sure, it had hurt that Peter left her in the lurch with a child on the way, but that was more pride than any love. She hadn't had any deep feelings for him in years. "I don't know, to be honest. I would think 'Peter' would be fine. Did you want to talk to him? He's in the family room, I think."

Justin crunched his chips and darted his gaze everywhere but at her. Was he thinking he'd be betraying her if he went and talked to Peter? Was he nervous that Peter might not like him? This whole idea was feeling worse and worse as the moments dragged on. But then Justin surprised her. "Yeah, I think I should go talk to him, so he can see that I'm okay and that you did a great job raising me even if he couldn't be here to help out."

She had a fantastic kid. "Okay, we can go find him."

Claudia ignored Zoe's pointed stare and fake cough as she left her plate on the coffee table and took Justin's hand. He must have been almost as nervous as she was, since his hand was sweaty and he actually let her hold it. He hadn't wanted to hold her hand since he was six. "It's going to be fine, hon."

"Oh, I know," he said, his voice much more confident than the sweat on his hand revealed. "I just hope I like him."

That was a perfect attitude to take into this encounter. She wished her mind wasn't running to "I hope he doesn't think I'm a fat cow."

****

Claudia stood back from the scene unfolding before her and let her son do the talking, but she was there right behind him if he needed her. So far, she hadn't had to say a thing, even though Peter kept flicking glances at her.

Justin hovered on the arm of the big chair Peter sat in. As he explained the intricacies of his latest video game and the way Nate didn't always let him win, since it was good for his character, Justin kept his arms crossed over his chest. But it was less a protective gesture and more a pride in himself and relaxation. He'd jumped into the conversation with Peter as if they were old friends and Justin had every right to his undivided attention.

Fortunately, Peter hadn't been talking to anyone at the time, so Claudia didn't have to deal with Justin being rude and butting in once he got his mind set on something.

"So anyway, there's this level on Spiderman that you have to swing left and right and not miss a single thing while picking up clues. I scored on it, and it was so cool. I can't wait to get to the next level."

Peter hadn't said much yet, but Justin hadn't exactly given him a chance. He looked a little bewildered, though he was at least paying attention. "How many levels are you talking?"

"Probably about twenty or more, I think. I didn't look at the back of the package yet, or even get cheat codes off the Internet, since we're trying to beat it on our own." Justin shrugged. "So anyway, I just wanted to tell you that I think it's great meeting you, and thanks for being with my mom to make me."

Claudia felt her breath back up in her throat. The expression on her face most likely closely mirrored the dawning look of horror on Peter's face.

And Justin went on. "She hasn't really explained the whole baby thing to me yet, so I'm not sure what all was involved, but I hope it was fun, since I'm fun."

Open up, floor, and swallow her whole. Yet she still couldn't get her mouth to do anything but open and close.

"If you've ever been worried that Mom wasn't going to do a good job with me, you can stop now. She's the best in the world, even if she won't let me call you a sperm donor, and I think it's cool to finally meet you. I mean, how many people get to go back to school tomorrow and say, 'Hey, I finally got to meet my dad and he was pretty cool'? Ought ta be fun. I'm going to go get some more soda, Mom. I'll see you later, Peter. I want to tell Grandpa about this awesome basket I made at church this morning. Have fun, and it was nice meeting you." Justin trotted off toward the kitchen.

Peter gave a vague wave of his hand before shaking his head and looking at Claudia. She swallowed nervously, still not sure what to say, if she should apologize or if she should just ride the wave. Although that had gone a whole lot better than she had thought possible.

It could have been worse, anyway.

"Wow." Peter wiped his fingers across the top of his mouth. It was a nervous gesture from years ago, and it tugged at her a little.

"Yeah, he's, um, something else, huh?" Claudia remained standing even though it made her feel awkward to tower over him in her three-inch heels. After the flats had gone into the fire the moment she got home from her date with Eddie, she'd worn only heels. They gave her a height advantage right now, but it seemed silly to force it—until he stood up and took her hand, leaving her at his eye level.

"He is something, Claudia. You did a good job."

Well, that wasn't quite the response she'd been prepared for. And now what did she say since the verbal ball was back in her court? "Um, thank you." So weak, but she couldn't think of anything else on such short notice. She couldn't even dredge up all the old feelings of abandonment to blast him with.

"Well, I think Brad's waving me over, so I'll be

going."

He ducked out before she could say anything else, and it was a letdown to not have said anything but, "Um, thanks." She looked around the room but couldn't find Justin, and she didn't want to face Zoe just yet. She could go talk to her parents. She hadn't seen them since the buffet line. When she looked around for them, though, they seemed to be in a pretty intense conversation with their heads close together. Maybe not.

May's smiling face greeted her when she walked back into the dining room with the intention of maybe grabbing more potato salad, the great equalizer of confusion. She wished it was a chocolate cake. Maybe that would come later. She hadn't been able to make herself bake a cake for this supposed celebration, but she would when it was all said and done.

"How are you doing?" May asked.

Claudia had stuffed some potato salad in her mouth and chewed for a while before swallowing. It gave her a chance to be as diplomatic as possible. "Fine. Everything was great. When does your dad want to start things?"

"Hopefully soon. Things are going well...so far. I don't want it to explode from prolonged exposure." May stared down at her clasped hands.

Claudia laughed and covered those hands with her own. "I can't say I would have asked for this, but it actually did turn out okay. Peter and I had our first adult conversation in years, and it went fine. He even met Justin and was impressed with him. He complimented me on raising a good kid." And hadn't that been strange?

May grabbed Claudia's hands and beamed at her. "Oh, that's wonderful. I'm so happy things worked out so well."

"I don't know if I'd say they worked out well, but they worked out." May's smile slipped, and Claudia wanted to take the qualifier back. What did it matter if May wanted everyone to act like a big happy family? Would it kill Claudia to let her have her delusions for one afternoon?

May held up a hand before Claudia could get word one out. "No, you're right. I was hoping for too much too soon. Sorry about that."

"It's okay, May. I know this is hard for you, harder since he seems to want to be a part of your family again. I just don't think I can let him be part of our family." She'd never been less than honest with May—except for that terrible period where May had worn green eye shadow with green eyeliner. But that was minor compared to this conversation. She had to be honest here. This wasn't merely a fashion faux pas. "If he wants to be involved with Justin, we'd have to talk about that a lot before it happened. But he didn't seem to want anything more than what Justin gave him, which was a little conversation and some insight into what a great kid he is."

"That's good. I'm glad, then. Do you know where he went? I wanted to make a little announcement."

May lowered her eyelashes, and Claudia knew something was up. She hoped it didn't have anything to do with her and Peter. "He went off with Brad, somewhere in the back of the house. They could be grunting over tools, for all I know." She did not want to offer to go find them. She'd done her good deed for the day by staying in this house with Peter and eating lunch despite his presence. She didn't need to go any further.

May wandered off with a slight smile on her face. Something was definitely up.

Ten minutes later Claudia waited in the family room with everyone else to find out what that secret smile had been about.

"We have an announcement to make," Brad said, banging a plastic spoon against his plastic cup.

"That's not very effective," Peter said from the other side of the room.

Claudia's gaze was drawn to him against her will. He was still a very good-looking man. He also had a magnetism that couldn't be ignored, even if he had always been used to getting his way.

The conversation continued around them with all the adults jabbering away. Claudia put two fingers in her mouth and whistled. That stopped everyone in their conversational tracks. She smiled and waved a hand at May, grateful that, despite the magnetism, she felt nothing at all for Peter.

"Thanks, Claudia. I forgot you could do that."

"No prob, May. I don't get to use it often anymore."

The small crowd laughed as Justin mumbled, "Yeah, right," loud enough for everyone to hear.

Brad took the floor again and raised his plastic cup. "I'd like to thank all of you for coming. Today is a special day for more reasons than you know. Tell them, May."

Eyes shining bright and hands clasped over her abdomen, May said, "We're having a baby."

Brad grabbed her up as if she weighed nothing and

twirled her around while she laughed like a loon. Everyone crowded in to tell the soon-to-be parents how exciting this was. Claudia hung back for a moment so Brad's parents could get to her first. And then May's father rose from his chair to hug her. Claudia looked away for a moment, knowing that she might not make it through seeing such happiness when her own expecting news had been met only with anger almost eleven years ago. While this wouldn't be Roger's first grandchild, it would be the first to be a happy blessing from day one. As much as Roger now loved Justin, it wasn't going to be the same situation. Everyone had been hoping May would get pregnant soon. And now she was.

Brad finally put May down when she threatened to throw up on him. Justin was yelling that this was fantastic because now they could all ruffle someone else's hair, since there would be a new baby in the family. Zoe said something about not needing a dog now, and Claudia's gaze caught on Peter's.

That's how it should have happened for her, too, all those years ago. Pregnancy was a wonderful thing. Bringing another life into the world was fantastic. But at eighteen and barely out of high school, she had known it wasn't quite what her parents hoped for her. And then Peter turned away from her and continued to make his plans for college as if nothing earth-shattering had happened. She looked down at her shoes and swallowed back unexpected tears. She was so happy for May and Brad. They'd been trying for the last three years for a baby. No way was she going to ruin this for them by wishing anyone would have been this excited for her when she got pregnant.

Something drew her gaze back to Peter at that

moment, and it was as if eleven years evaporated and left them able to read each other's minds again, finish each other's sentences. And if she wasn't mistaken, he was regretting it, too.

Chapter Seven

"May, that was delicious. Thank you." Claudia got up and started clearing paper plates and used plastic ware after they'd had cake and mimosas to celebrate the great news. May had just had a flute of orange juice.

"Here, let me help you with that." Peter got up from the table and gathered his father's plate, his own, and Brad's.

Before she could protest, he led the way into the kitchen. Left with plates in her hands and a sinking feeling in her heart, she didn't have much choice but to follow unless she wanted to look like an idiot by putting the plates back down and sitting in her chair like a petulant child.

But walking across the dining room and into the kitchen was the second hardest walk of the day. Zoe was caught in conversation with May and neither seemed to realize what had happened. Which left her to walk on her own.

Once inside the kitchen with the door gently swinging shut behind her, she placed the plates in the trash can and turned to go back out as quickly as she could. Peter caught her arm before she made it two steps from the trash.

"Claudia."

She stared down at his hand on her arm. His tanned flesh looked odd against her winter-white skin. And yet that used to make them laugh. They'd compare how she never tanned to how he could be a burnished gold within days of summer starting.

The moment lasted too long with her continuing not to look up, but keeping her eyes on his hand.

He backed up. "Sorry."

Finally she looked up at him and struggled to find some trace of the boy who had taken her virginity in the back of the Mustang he'd received from his dad before he went off to college and a career in business.

She waited for him to say more. Crossing her arms over her chest, she stood as still as she could and tried to mentally prepare herself for whatever it was he needed to say.

"That should have been how it was for you, and I should have been more mature."

She didn't move a muscle. Peter didn't say he was sorry, and he certainly didn't admit he'd done something wrong. "Should" didn't mean shit to her. "What does that do for me?"

He dropped his gaze and seemed to have a great fascination with the tiles on the floor.

She hadn't wanted to bring Justin up again. They'd talked enough earlier. As much time as she'd been willing to give the subject. She'd be just as happy if Peter decided not to try to see Justin again at all while he was here. And now she had to deal with the fact that he had seen him and was offering her something she'd never thought she'd get. "I asked you a question." And she wasn't budging until she got some answers.

He ran a rough hand through his perfect dark hair but wouldn't look up.

She fought the ridiculous urge to bend down to

make eye contact.

He saved her from embarrassing herself by finally looking up and piercing her with the eyes so like her son's. "I should never have left the way I did or gotten angry at you for what I saw as you getting yourself pregnant and trying to ruin everything for me just when I was about to get started with my life." His words came out haltingly and unsure. It was not reassuring.

"I didn't do it on my own." Why was she pursuing this conversation at all? She needed to move out of the kitchen, finish collecting trash, and take her son home where they could resume their own life.

"I know that. Your mom pulled me aside earlier and asked me not to interfere in your lives since you've been doing fine on your own. She said he may look like me, but he's nothing like me as a person. That he already has more honor at ten than I ever did."

Oh, that probably had gone over like a fly in the cake batter. "And?" She couldn't help it. There had to be more, and she needed to hear it.

"And I didn't really say anything to her. I didn't know what to say. I can't believe how much he looks like me."

"He does look a lot like you." She tried to make a joke and take back control of the conversation. "How is it that I did all the work, and he looks nothing like me? Shouldn't I have at least gotten a nose or a chin for all my efforts?"

He put his hand on her arm again, and her weak laughter stopped in mid-ha.

"You shouldn't have had to do it all by yourself. I know that now. And I want to make it up to you."

She took a step back, breaking the contact, but

coming up against the wall. If he came any closer, she'd have nowhere to escape. "There's nothing to make up, Peter. He's a great kid and my pride and joy." She couldn't help it if she'd put more emphasis on the word "my." But she did feel a slight pang in her chest when he winced.

"Yeah, your kid." His fingers speared through his hair again, and it stood up on end before he smoothed it. "Anyway, I would like to make it up to you. I didn't even pay you child support, and you never asked for anything."

She didn't need anything from him. It was on the tip of her tongue to say so, but he was still talking.

"I was a horrible person. I should have stayed. I should have done a lot of things I didn't do." Backing up, he rested his rear end on the butcher block but didn't break eye contact. "Isn't this where you berate me and tell me how horrible things have been and what an unmitigated jerk I am?"

"No, actually, this is where I tell you that I adore Justin with everything I have and if I had it all to do over again, I wouldn't change a thing. I love him. He's my whole world. He's a joy when he's not being a typical boy, and he's smart. Your money or your guilt won't change any of that."

The kitchen door creaked open and Zoe peeked her head in.

"Go away," Claudia said when her sister opened her mouth. "I've got this."

The door creaked back closed after Zoe shot Peter one last evil eye.

"Your sister doesn't like me very much."

"She has nothing to do with this conversation. You

wanted to talk about Justin. Let's talk about Justin."

He pulled at the collar at his throat. "I don't know if I want to talk about Justin. I only wanted to tell you I realize I made a mistake, and I'm sorry for not being there for you and him."

Here was a moment she could back down from or take as an opportunity. She took the opportunity because she didn't know if she'd ever get another like it. He seemed so open right now, and he was never a very open kind of guy. Witness ten years of silence. "It's not the money or not being here that was the problem. I knew you had your whole future planned out, and a kid thrown into the mix didn't sit well with your dad."

"He—"

"No, let me finish." She drew a deep breath and fought swatting him with her hand. Why did everyone always want to interrupt her? "The bigger part was cutting yourself off altogether. I'll admit I might not have been open to anything when Justin was first born and you left, but you could have come back and tried again. There are plenty of fathers out there who are only peripherally involved in their child's life, and you could have been one of them." She zeroed in on him. "It wasn't easy for me, but I'm not going to let you waltz in and start taking over things now."

May popped into the kitchen and ignored Peter's raised eyebrows. "Claudia, I need you back out in the living room. Zoe's about to go kamikaze on Brad's friend Dex, who just showed up, and you're the only one who can calm her down. She's muttering something about pruning him, and it doesn't look good."

Claudia sighed, knowing the conversation with Peter was over and she probably wouldn't have a chance to get back to it. But at least she'd been able to get her remarks in. It had gone better than she could have hoped. She'd have to settle for that. For now.

"Lead the way. God knows she can't seem to handle herself right now with the whole Casanova thing."

****

After calming down Zoe and sending her upstairs for a timeout until the infamous Dex left, Claudia had an overwhelming urge to find Nate. May had said he was going to be here a little late, and Claudia sure could use him now. As if she'd conjured him, he strode in through the back door.

His light hair was swept back from his forehead. The wind followed him in and stirred the air in the kitchen. He looked like salvation and yumminess all wrapped in one.

Something snapped inside her, an elemental something that told her to stop pussyfooting around and go after what she wanted. With that in mind, she strode right up to him and grabbed his arm.

But she faltered at the pitying smile on his face when she got so close. After years and years together, virtually in each other's pockets, she knew each and every expression his face could twist itself into—from happy to silly, from mad to totally pissed. They all held subtle differences, but she could tell. And this one said he knew things were hard having Peter here and he was by her side. He'd help her through this as he had every other thing in her life. But she didn't want to lean on him. She didn't want him to think of her as a helpless person who needed him to save her. She wanted him to think of her as an independent woman who wanted his hot body.

She tried to wrap a hand around his wrist to bring it to her lips and kiss his palm, but he patted her head instead and gave her that smile again.

She almost gave in to the childish urge to step on his foot. But that wasn't going to further her cause, either. Taking a deep breath, she centered herself while trying to remember what Zoe had said about flirting. It was lowering to have to take her younger sister's advice, but if it worked Claudia would just claim it as her own inspiration.

She sidled up to him, ran a hand up the buttons of his shirt and gave him a sultry wink when he glanced down at her. She ignored the baffled look on his face and soldiered on. She was going to see this through even if it killed her libido.

Justin chose that moment to walk into the kitchen. He took one look at Claudia wrapped around Nate, snickered, and ran back out.

Nate stiffened under Claudia's hand, but she wasn't letting go. She figured she had about twenty seconds before someone came rushing in to see if she really truly was clinging to Nate like a vine.

So she took advantage of her small amount of time and boldly laid her lips right on his. Let him try to offer her first aid for that.

****

Nate stood stock still for a moment while the warmth of Claudia's lips heated to scalding. Her tongue probed the seam of his mouth, trying to gain entrance. The feel of her pressed against him flamed through his blood and would have set him back on his ass if he hadn't grabbed onto her hips with both hands, sinking his fingers into the flesh there and feeling the rasp of her dress against the calluses on his palms.

She drew him in, and he forgot who precisely he was kissing in the meeting of their lips, the wild feel of her in his arms. For a second she was just a woman, not a mother, not his best friend, not the girl he'd stood by all those years ago when she was pregnant. A woman who was making him forget every thought in his head. But then it all came back to him in an excruciating instant, and his fingers pushed instead of pulled, trying to get away instead of holding fast.

Her lips were swollen and her skin flushed. Moisture glistened on the crest of her upper lip, and it was all he could do not to rub his finger just there to see how truly soft she was.

But, between one ragged breath and the next, his gut churned. He couldn't do this. He couldn't let her be anything more than his best friend. A friend he wouldn't lose to his lust. Or hers.

He walked out the door before he could change his mind.

****

"Argh!" Claudia was grateful for the empty apartment when she crashed through the door and slammed her purse onto the front entryway table. "Could that have been any better or gone any worse?" She'd stayed at May's long enough to find out that Justin's grandfather wanted to give him a vintage collection of baseball cards and a ball he'd caught during some long-ago World Series game. She'd left without another word from anyone, avoiding the grasp of Peter's hand as he'd tried to head her off at the door. She'd had no patience left and little enough time to breathe before she feared she'd cry over Nate's abrupt rejection.

Feeling a particular violence welling up inside her, she kicked the side table, then hobbled around on her injured toes.

All she'd wanted was a little nookie. All she'd wanted was to continue to feel the absolute thrill that shot up her spine when Nate's fingers had dug into her hips, pulling her closer to him, as if he wanted to pull her inside him.

But then everything had changed.

He'd shoved her away like she had the plague or something. And had taken off as if she was going to drag him to the ground and make him gnaw his own arm off to get away from her. Was she that repulsive? Was it so out of the realm of possibility that she might have some needs as a woman? Something that had nothing to do with being a mother or a friend? Something that was all female and all sexual? All she'd wanted was a little icing, and she'd got nothing, not even a piece of stale cake.

Throwing herself on the couch, she wondered what she'd done wrong. Then again, maybe he hadn't wanted her at all. Maybe he really did only think of her as an asexual person who was his best friend and nothing more.

But the sizzle of that kiss was hard to miss. At least until he had pushed her away. Damn.

A knock sounded on the door, startling her out of the doldrums. Justin had gone home from the luncheon with his grandma and grandpa and was due back any time, according to the big clock in the kitchen.

She composed her features with a great deal of effort. The very last thing she wanted to do was explain her mood to her son. Or her mother, for that matter. Her mother who had nagged her about dating Nate for years but then had seemed to get the hint, only to start setting her up with completely boring guys.

Reasonably sure she had things under control, she took care opening the door, not wanting to yank it off its hinges.

Claudia didn't even let Nate draw a breath when she opened the door. She swooped in on him, capturing his mouth with hers. She planted one on him like she'd never planted before. He wasn't going to get away from her this time. His interest, or lack of it, be damned.

He kicked the door shut behind him and twirled her around to press her back against the wood. Snaking his arms around her waist, he held on tight, pressing her curves up against his chest and stomach, melding her thighs to his, thrusting his tongue into her open mouth and taking command of the kiss.

He turned her so he rested against the door. She wasn't sure her knees would hold her up while he plundered and took, giving back in kind. But his arms locked around her kept her upright. For now, at least.

****

Nate's mind whirled while his hands roamed up Claudia's back and cupped the base of her skull, changing the angle of the kiss. She followed his lead. Her fingers crept into his short hair and played with the neckline his barber had put there just the other day. The exposed skin was tender and sensitive. Her light touch sent a shudder through his body and had his cock swelling in his pants. She must have felt him getting hard, because she gasped into his mouth and snuggled up closer, cradling him against her stomach.

He slipped his hands up under her hair, loving the way the strands sifted through his fingers and clung to the calluses on his palms. He changed the angle yet again. Tilting her back just a little, he pressed his hand to her spine, wishing she wore a shirt instead of this dress. He wanted to feel her flesh under his now that he'd let himself get a taste of her lips. He swept his hand from her spine to her butt and reached for the hem.

She surprised him by revealing a hidden zipper on her side. Yanking it down, she then shoved his hand into the opening and pressed it to her tightly beaded nipples under her satiny bra. Something about this whole thing felt illicit, but when she pressed more fully into his palm, he could do nothing less than feel her.

"God, yes, Nate." She moaned into his mouth then nibbled on his tongue. He was so hard in his pants he could have drilled a hole in the wall.

But her voice snapped inside him. He leaned his forehead against hers, keeping just far enough away to feel her breath feathering his lips. "You're my friend. I shouldn't be doing this."

Her fingers speared through the short sides of his hair, and she grabbed his ears. Yanking his head up, she stared into his eyes. "Don't you dare get all noble on me now. I want you to take me and take me hard. Forget everything else and feel me." She let go of his ears, pulling her dress farther up her thighs and tugging it to her waist. The fabric at her side gaped, leaving one breast peeking out through the hole.

Despite his thoughts to the contrary just a minute ago, he could in fact do this, his mouth watering at the duskiness of her nipple barely cresting the demi cup of her bra. He'd die if he didn't take the pebble into his mouth and suck it for all he was worth.

And he wasn't planning on dying today. Though he was apparently going to heaven.

Her skin in his mouth was the best thing he'd ever tasted. The faint vanilla trailing on her skin made him wild. He drew and drew on her breast, listening to her moans and words of ecstasy. With her skirt bunched up around her waist, he could also reach other parts of her, as close to heaven as he figured he'd ever get.

He trailed a finger up the inside of her leg, lingering at the lace holding up her thigh-high stockings. That small strip of lace and elastic made him mad for more. When he finally found his way to the soft skin beside the edge of her panties, he had a brief flash of not being able to go on. But Claudia disabused him of that notion right away when she thrust her pelvis into his hand and he felt the silky wetness dampening her panties.

He gave out a groan that she answered.

"God, you're so wet."

"Take me." Her hands fisted in his hair and dragged his mouth back up to hers.

Her hips were restless under his probing fingers. She took one and then two with ease. Her inner walls squeezed him as her tongue thrust deep into his mouth. She was wild, and he wanted her more than he'd wanted anything in his entire life.

"Come for me," he whispered in her ear, licking the delicate shell, loving the moans that were growing louder with every circle of his index finger. "Come for me."

"No." She tossed her head back and forth. "I want you inside me when I come for the first time."

"But I want you wetter." He drove her relentlessly, pinning her to him with his forearm. He wasn't going to let her get away from him until he'd made her scream his name.

And then she did. And that one word had never sounded so good in all his life.

She panted with her head resting on his shoulder. He could definitely get used to this. Who knew his best friend was so passionate? He shunted the distinction off to the side of his mind. Right now he didn't hold Claudia his friend in his arms, but Claudia the woman, who he was sure could take him to heights he'd never reached before.

He was ready to pick her up and toss her over his shoulder to head to the bedroom when knocking filled his head.

She broke away, a glazed look in her eyes. "I should get that," she whispered from bee-stung lips, swollen and glistening from his kisses. Her eyes nearly rolled in panic. "It might be Justin and my parents."

As if on cue, the pipsqueak's voice came loud through the door. "Come on, Mom! I have to pee, and Grandma forgot her key. Hurry!"

"You better get that," he murmured. He was reluctant to release her, but he couldn't let his little buddy see him in this compromising position. Until he knew what the hell was going on for himself, he didn't want anyone to see him this close to Claudia. "I'll go in your room and wait for your mom to leave, if you want.

You may not be able to explain your swollen lips when I'm standing right here."

Pulling down her dress and zipping up the zipper, she shot him a grateful look, but it was tinged with confusion. Yeah, he didn't know what the hell was going on, either. He bumped into the arched doorway on his way to Claudia's bedroom, not sure that it was his best choice. But, for better or worse, he'd made the decision and couldn't go back. All along the hallway, he wondered what the hell had just happened. He had a hard on for his best friend in the world. It was either his very best idea or the worst mistake he'd ever made.

****

"So, Justin didn't say much on the car ride over here," Mona Bradley said as soon as she walked through the door of Claudia's apartment.

Claudia had been dreading this, not sure what she was going to hear, or even what the outcome was. She hadn't been able to get Justin alone after her conversation with Peter because he'd decided to ride home with Grandma and Grandpa and play for a while. She'd used the time to roam around the streets in her car, but it hadn't improved her mood at all. But those kisses from Nate and the orgasm that had blown her mind had gone a long way toward making her feel like she could float straight up to the sky. She couldn't think about that now, though, because her mom might catch a hint of what was going on. She couldn't afford that at the moment.

After putting down her purse and taking off her light jacket, Mona looked around the living room. She chose a seat on the couch, and Claudia prayed she wasn't settling in for a long talk. She certainly didn't want to talk about too much with Nate hovering in her room. There were many things her mother could blurt out that would embarrass the hell out of her. And she didn't want to give him time to rummage around through her things, if she could help it. She certainly didn't want him to find her trusty vibrator and know how truly dry her dry spell had been lately.

Justin had already breezed by, shooting straight for the bathroom. "Hi, Mom. Bye, Mom. Gotta go!"

Claudia shook her head at the boy's bladder and said, "What do you mean, you couldn't get him to say anything?" Really, with Justin, it could be anything or nothing.

"Well, honey, I don't know how to tell you this."

It occurred to Claudia to let her mom off the hook, but then sometimes life's little joys came from putting your parents in uncomfortable positions. She was perverse like that. Plus, if it was something else, she wanted to hear all about it. "You can tell me anything. What did he do now?"

"Do?" Mona's clear brow wrinkled. "Oh, he didn't do anything."

"For once?"

Mona laughed. "Yeah, for once, he was actually quite the ideal grandchild for a whole afternoon. I was surprised myself. But what happened earlier at May's lunch could account for that model behavior."

So it was Peter. Claudia sat down to hear exactly what had happened. She didn't know if she could take it standing up. "Did he say anything at all? I couldn't corner him after he met Peter, no matter how much I tried."

"Did you talk to him before the lunch at all?

Prepare him for what it was going to be like to meet his father when he can't even remember him?"

And just like that, Claudia was thrown on the defensive. Something about her mom's tone didn't sit right with her. "I found out only a few days ago from May that Peter had come home to help out with his father for a short time."

Mona twitched on the couch, facing Claudia head on. "I don't know what you had expected, but we probably shouldn't have gone there. He hardly had anything to say to the poor boy. Even the few words he spoke were vague enough to be from a complete stranger. I probably iced half of the food May laid out while I stared him down."

"Oh, Mom. He is a complete stranger."

"Don't 'oh, Mom' me. A body has a right to absolutely loathe the boy who left you. And you don't seem too worried about it." Her mom stared at her over the tops of her glasses and looked none too happy. "You seem pretty nonchalant, actually, for how much you used to curse him to hell and back."

"Mom! Let's not talk about that right now. I don't want Justin to overhear us bashing his biological father." Not to mention having Nate in her bedroom. If he'd left the door ajar and listened hard, he could probably overhear every single word.

"Justin said he was going to go straight to his room after the bathroom because he had a project to work on. I told him to go for it, since I didn't want him to hear you swearing if you were so inclined." She cocked an eyebrow and tapped a finger on the arm of the couch. "In fact, you don't look like you're going to bust a gasket at all. You look fine with my little revelation.

Why is that?"

"Peter says he wants to help me out, pay child support, or do anything he can to make up for leaving us and continuing with his life as if nothing happened."

"No!"

"Yes!" Claudia was mocking her mom and got swatted on the arm for her impertinence.

"I can't believe he's still alive after you got through with him. Did he try to sway you at all?"

Man, she must have really been carrying around a grudge if so many people thought she should have taken him apart limb by limb because he was breathing the Pennsylvania air again. "He did try to talk to me—"

"And you cut him down with your razor tongue?"

"Now you sound just like Zoe." The women of her family were bloodthirsty. "No, I did nothing of the sort. Actually, he apologized for the way he acted when I told him I was pregnant, and for not being here for Justin and me when we were younger."

"And you believed that tripe?"

"Oh, Mom," Claudia said again and sighed. She leaned back in her chair. "I have to say, it soothed my ego to finally have him apologize. But do I believe him?" She sighed again and moved her hair off her forehead. "I think it's convenient for him to look back and regret it. But I doubt it will change anything at all."

"Just as long as you don't fall for it—and for him—again, I'm sure you'll be fine." Mona peeked around the corner. "Since Justin's still in the bathroom, I guess now is a good time to tell you he has something different to talk with you about."

"What now? I don't know if I can handle any more."

"Oh, it's nothing bad. But I think you might need Nate for it."

Yeah, she needed Nate for quite a few things lately. Knowing he was most likely sitting on the edge of her bed right now shot a thrill straight to her core. But she couldn't show her mom.

And whatever it was with Justin, she would handle it, just like she handled everything else.

Chapter Eight

Nate was indeed sitting on the edge of Claudia's bed. He tried not to slide off the slippery satin bedspread, and tried not to think about everything his traitorous body had wanted to do with Claudia not twenty minutes ago. To say it was weird to think about getting Claudia naked in here—or anywhere, for that matter—was a gross understatement. Sure, once or twice, years ago, he'd thought about trying to take her out, date her. And his mom, for as much as she moved outside of herself every once in a while in the intervening years, would make comments about him just finally marrying Claudia and making the boy his own. But he'd never really considered anything of the sort himself since she'd gotten pregnant.

He'd been there for her when that rat bastard Peter had left her alone at three months pregnant. He'd been outside the delivery room, where he'd had to shut his ears to Claudia's snarling and yelling while giving birth to Justin. And yeah, he loved the ten-year-old who brightened his day and his life. But Nate had always thought of himself as a fond uncle. He didn't know whether he ever wanted to be a dad, much less be responsible for a wife with a child born from someone else.

Not that he wouldn't. But it was a big step away from the single, total-bachelor life Nate had enjoyed for himself all these years and envisioned continuing indefinitely. He chased after some women, dated, satisfied his urges and theirs. But he never really gave himself to any of them. He didn't know if he ever could. And until that episode out in the living room, the way Claudia had come apart in his arms, the episode he was still trying to calm his hormones after, he hadn't thought that was a problem. Now his head was filled with turmoil and his heart didn't know what he should do.

And if Claudia didn't get rid of her mom soon and rescue him from this very feminine room where he couldn't stop thinking about the bed under him, he might go stark raving mad.

It was uncanny the way things happened in his life. Just as he was about to start poking through things in this room where he'd never before entered, Claudia showed up in the doorway with her finger to her closed mouth.

"Come on out," she whispered through lips no longer swollen.

He followed her out, slightly wistful for what he could have done to her on that bed. But he was still having a difficult time thinking of it being Claudia under him. Claudia! His best friend. Too weird.

He continued following her out to the deck she'd had built onto the back of the house, above the back door to the store. Big buckets of flowers lined the corners of the structure, filling the air with a sweet fragrance that matched whatever she was wearing tonight on her soft skin. Tiny twinkling lights wrapped around the railing, giving off soft light that spilled over the half-closed blooms. A little patio table with four chairs dominated the small space, with a fat candle squatting in the middle of the tabletop.

She grabbed a lighter from a box near the door and lit the wick, then took a seat at the table, gesturing for him to take the seat next to her. He chose the one across from her instead, thinking it would better if she wasn't in touching distance while they discussed whatever she had on her mind.

She pouted. There was no other word for the expression on her face, but it was one he didn't think he'd ever seen on her before.

"You don't want to sit next to me? I won't bite unless you ask. Nicely."

His brain shorted out. Claudia, his best friend, was offering to bite him? He cleared his throat and tried to get his brain back online. Christ. This was not easy. It was going to take a little time to readjust his thinking. In the meantime he readjusted his pants and the way he was sitting to relieve a little of the tension swelling down there.

"I'm just going to sit over here." He cleared his throat, again, thankful that at least his mouth was working the right way.

"Are you sure?" She batted her lashes at him and a flash of memory hit him in the gut. He'd offered her first aid for her eye just the other day for that. Had she been trying to flirt with him then? Oh, man, that must have crushed her. Should he apologize?

But before he could make a decision, she went on, oblivious to his turmoil.

"I just told Justin to clean up his room before dinner, so we have about ten minutes to talk." She sat back in her cushioned chair and crossed her arms under her rather impressive chest. The nipple he'd licked and sucked seemed to call to him even from across the distance.

But, God, did that make him feel lower than dirt to even be thinking about her boobs. This was not going to work. It was just too weird for words. "What is going on?"

It was a pretty blunt question, but Claudia stepped up to the plate without a single hesitation. "I want icing."

What? He breathed in through his nose and tried to let the flowers around him calm him. It didn't work, nor did it make anything make any more sense. "So go down to the grocery store and buy yourself a can. It's like two bucks or something. I'll give you the money."

She laughed, throwing her head back. The twinkling lights picked up the glow of her skin. His mouth watered, against his better judgment.

"Not that kind of icing. And actually, I just want some cake. I've decided to start eating cake again instead of stale cookies. And you are definitely the person I want to give it to me."

This was not making one whit of sense to him. Had she gone off the deep end after seeing Peter and didn't know it? And the way she'd worded the thing about him giving it to her made him think she was on the verge of something he might not approve of at all.

And then she proceeded to blow him away. And not in a good way.

"I want icing in my life. I want the sparks. I want to be able to wear high heels and feel like a woman. I don't want to have to follow a schedule or wait to be talked to. I don't want to be talked down to or told that my cake business is a hobby I have to give up when I get shackled to a short, toupee-wearing idiot."

Her eyes were bright and her hair nearly wild. But now he finally understood what was behind all this. Kind of. But what did it have to do with him?

"So you want icing? Or cake? Or both? What?" he asked, crossing his arms over his chest and leaning back in his own chair. And what exactly did that have to do with kissing him, coming for him while she called his name? All things he was raring to do again, but shouldn't be. Damn. This could be interesting.

She began drawing invisible pictures on the table with her fingertip. He could almost feel it on his skin.

"I just want some cake in my life. I think I *rate* some cake in my life. I don't need the whole enchilada, with the icing and the sparks and the undying love, but I would like *some* sparks, *some* heat, *some* good sex." She fisted her hand at her chest and he knew she meant business.

"And I fit into all this how?"

Her smile was the closest thing to predatory he'd ever seen outside the big cat display at the zoo. "Why, you're going to be the cake, and from what we did less than half an hour ago, I'd say you're going to like it."

****

"I can call Nate, honey, but I'm pretty sure that's the night he's out of town for business," Claudia said that evening as she arranged on a roll some of the lunchmeat May had sent home with her and slathered the mayonnaise on thick like Justin liked it. The boy was really into his condiments. The idea of a girls' night had been a good one earlier in the day, but both May and Zoe had ended up having to call off. Zoe had forgotten she had a date, and May had said later would be a better time. Claudia tried not to feel blown off, but it was a close thing.

"We should have asked him while he was here earlier," she said now. Not that she could have remembered in the afterglow of that orgasm.

"I want him to go."

"And I'm sure he wants to go, but there's no guarantee he can. He does have a life of his own, you know." Claudia rubbed the base of her skull and moved to put everything back in the refrigerator. She'd lost her appetite about the time Justin had asked, right after Nate had driven off, if Nate could please take him to the annual father-son dinner. Every year she'd been his substitute dad, but apparently that wasn't going to work this year.

She understood. She did. And tried not to make it about her or her simple lack of a penis when that had been okay for the last five years. But it did still hurt. Just a little.

"Well, can we call him? I want to ask him before he makes a date with some girl or something."

Claudia's heart clenched. Justin had walked out to the deck right after she made her announcement to Nate that he was going to be her cake. He hadn't said anything after that to her, as Justin had started yammering. Then Nate left, saying nothing other than goodbye as he walked out the door without looking her in the eye.

Had she miscalculated? She probably should have asked him if he was dating someone before she started batting her eyelashes at him and kissing him, letting him take her straight to the moon and back. But they'd never really shared much about their love lives with one another. They could, and did, talk about nearly everything else, but that was one subject they each seemed to keep to themselves.

"I'll go call him," she said, when she realized she'd taken too long to answer and Justin was staring at her as if she had three heads. "You get your shower and then bring your homework out."

Picking up the phone from the kitchen, she hesitated over the keypad. She felt almost weird calling the man she'd talked to every day for years. She needed to get over this and figure out if she should do a full frontal assault again or look for her cake elsewhere.

The phone rang four times, and she was about to click the End button when he picked up.

"Hello?"

Her breath became shorter, hearing his rumbly voice across the line. Her palms were sweating, and she wondered briefly if she was in the middle of a panic attack.

"Hello? Is anyone there, or were you just planning on heavy breathing in my ear?"

Her heart fluttered damn near out of her chest.

"Last chance, sick puppy. I can hear you breathing, so unless you have something to say, I'm hanging up."

And then all she heard was a click as the line went dead. She'd never been more thankful Nate was one of the few holdouts on Caller ID. At least she didn't run the risk of him knowing it had been her.

Now all she had to decide was whether to call him back right away and pretend nothing had happened, or to wait a little bit, make sure Justin was starting his bath, then call and act as if nothing happened. She opted for number one, since it would mean getting the whole thing out of the way. And she wasn't much of a procrastinator.

Plus, she could hear the shower running down the hall, and Justin would yell if she walked in now and saw him naked. Boys—kids, for that matter. It wasn't like he had anything she hadn't seen before. Hell, she used to wipe his little butt for him for almost three full years.

And now she was procrastinating, again. She pressed the Talk button and then Redial. Putting the phone up to her ear, she waited for the ringing to start and mentally rehearsed what she would say to Nate.

But no ringing sounded in her ear. The only thing she heard was Nate's deep voice saying, "Well, hello, Claudia, were you planning on talking to me this time or am I in for a little more heavy breathing?"

Claudia couldn't help the nervous laughter that burbled out of her throat. So much for staying anonymous. The luxury had been taken right out of her hands. "Hey, Nate. Um, no, no more heavy breathing. Sorry about that the first time, I was trying to listen for Justin getting in the shower and got distracted before you answered the phone."

"Sounds kind of like a load of crap." The smile in his voice was evident.

Yeah, the excuse sounded lame to her, too, but she wasn't going to explain herself further or even discuss that subject again. Ever, if she could help it. "Anyway, Justin has a father-son dinner coming up on Friday night that he wanted you to go to with him, and I was wondering if you were available." She worked hard to restrain her imagination as to what *she* would like him to be available for.

"As long as I don't have anything going on, it should be fine. Why isn't he taking you, like he has every other year?"

"For some reason I'm not enough, and he asked for you." It still broke her heart a little, but the way Nate stepped up to the plate immediately warmed those broken pieces. "It's on Friday. Will you pick him up? I'd like to get pictures of the two of you." She'd almost said her two handsome men, but stopped herself at the last second. That was close.

"Let me look at my calendar here a minute." He made humming noises low in his throat that came shooting through the phone and right down into Claudia from her ear to her toes. He'd made the same noise with her nipple sucked into his mouth.

Who knew humming could be such a turn-on? And since when did everything Nate did make her gooey inside? They'd been friends for years and she'd never had a dirty thought about him. Well, maybe one or two, but she'd never been this focused on him and aware of his every breath.

Fortunately, he broke her out of her lustful haze by talking. "Actually that'll be fine. It should be a blast. What time, and what do I have to wear?"

How about right here, right now, and absolutely nothing but a big old smile? She tried to regulate her uneven breathing when it threatened to chuff out of her with the force of a steam engine. "Great. Justin will be so pleased, and it's suit-and-tie. Thanks for doing this."

She said goodbye before she could get all sappy about him and the way he thought about Justin's needs and participated in his life. Or before she asked again if he wanted to be her cake. Maybe she had completely disgusted him with her suggestion and he really wasn't ready to buy into it. But that kiss he'd laid on her kept popping back into her head, too, and so did the way she'd screamed his name. There was no denying he'd had an erection that would no doubt satisfy her like nothing else. But couldn't guys get it up for almost any female? Way too much to think about.

If nothing else, at least she'd get to see him in a suit. The last time had been at May's wedding, three years ago, and she hadn't fully taken the time to truly admire him. She wouldn't miss out again.

After raiding the refrigerator looking for something to cool her off a little, Claudia sat at the kitchen table sipping a glass of iced tea. The shower down the hall had turned off some time ago, and now she could hear Justin knocking around in his room. The ceiling fan whirred in the relative stillness as she contemplated the darkening sky in the distance.

Her thoughts whirled and twirled in her head. What was she doing, looking for icing after all these years? She'd done fine for herself, even if she'd had little love outside of her family. Justin and she hadn't suffered much for it. Life went on, even if you had no one in your bed.

"Bring your homework out to the table," she called to Justin, more to distract herself than to make sure he actually did it. She wondered what torture she would have to endure in the name of schoolwork this evening as she threw a bag of popcorn into the microwave.

He was like a herd of elephants tramping down the hallway. Zoe was out this evening, doing heaven only knew what on her date. Claudia hadn't had time to talk to her, either. She was feeling out of sorts without that contact, especially after her conversation with Nate. There was something about his easy acceptance of taking Justin to the dinner that spoke to her heart—and to her libido.

And she needed to get her mind out of the gutter if she wanted to concentrate on whatever torture it was Justin needed to work on tonight.

He trundled toward the living room, books in hand. Following more sedately with the steaming bag of popcorn, she tried, again, to remember what kind of homework Justin had this evening. And when it came to her, she shivered with dread.

Long division.

With books already spread out in a jumble on the low coffee table, Justin pulled his assignment from the bottom of a hopelessly messy backpack and smoothed it flat with his small hands. Hands so much like his father's. What a shame. Just one more thing he didn't get from her.

She shook her head to clear it and focused on what she remembered about remainders and carrying numbers.

But before they got started, Justin turned to her with shining eyes. "So what did Nate say? Will he take me? Does he want to be my dad for the night?"

He was practically bouncing, and she was so happy she didn't have to disappoint him. "Turns out I was wrong about what days he's out of town. He's thrilled to take you. He said he can't wait." Yeah, in between laughing at her heavy breathing routine and the way she'd totally embarrassed herself with her lame excuse about being distracted by Justin's shower.

"Oh, yeah! I can't wait. This is going to be so much cooler than the last couple of years. Did he say he was going to dress up? Do you think we should be, like, coordinated or anything?" He clasped his hands in front of his chest and had the biggest grin on his face she'd seen in a long time.

Inside, she picked up the pieces of her cracked heart and tried to overlook the comment about the other years where she was his date. On the outside, she smiled, ruffled his hair, and told him, "We can decide all that later. We have a few days, but right now we have enough long division to make me feel like my eyes are going to bleed." Another feeling erupted inside her to override the hurt—happiness for how he responded to Nate. If, and it was a big if, she ever managed to get Nate to see her as an actual woman instead of reminding him she was the one who'd been his friend forever, at least she knew she'd have her son's complete approval of the man she wanted.

An hour later, as she listened to Justin preparing for bed, she leaned back on the sofa, glad she had survived this interminable day. The water running as he brushed his teeth, the thud of his feet as he went to his room, and the soft thump of music drifting down the hall soothed her. These were normal things. Things she was used to and that fit into her regular day. Nothing like the rest of the day had been, with one upheaval after another. Perhaps she should just forget today ever happened and start anew tomorrow. It wasn't a bad idea, as far as she was concerned.

Chapter Nine

Claudia could have laughed at her naiveté, a mere handful of days after long division, if she didn't want so badly to howl at the moon. She'd moped around for days, trying to get hold of Nate, but he wasn't answering his phone. He never had answered her cake question, and now she didn't think she wanted to bring it up again, in case she wasn't getting his subtle hint to drop the whole thing.

She'd tried to talk Zoe into calling him earlier. They still had to go over the build-out plans Nate had left at the apartment on Saturday. But Zoe was absolutely refusing, in retaliation for Claudia making her deal with Dex, the lawyer, and May wasn't in a position to make any final decisions, since her partnership was still up in the air.

Which left Claudia with a phone call to make. She had even briefly thought of letting her mom handle things, but she was afraid of what might come out of her mother's mouth.

She sighed, thinking that he hadn't even taken them out to dinner on Monday as he had promised. She had really screwed things up with those kisses and letting him give her an orgasm. Though she really couldn't regret that last one. It far out ranked anything her trusty vibrator could provide.

Grabbing up the phone, she punched out his

number before she could lose her nerve.

He picked up on the third ring. "I was just going to call you."

"I doubt that, since you've been avoiding me the last several days." She certainly hadn't meant to sound so sharp, had in fact meant to be nice and forget anything had happened this last week at all, from Zoe's very first mention of cake onward, but something inside her was playing the devil.

"I haven't been avoiding you."

"Yeah, right."

There was a long pause, and she thought he'd hung up on her until he cleared his throat. "Look, I wasn't avoiding you completely. Grandma Stelle had a doctor's appointment on Monday, and she's not doing so well. Mom is having fits, and I've been on the phone day and night with her, talking about nursing homes."

"That must have been fun. I bet Stelle is not liking that at all." Nate's grandma was stubborn to a fault, and she had always said she would die before she went to one of those "old folks' homes."

Claudia knew she should be relieved that he'd been preoccupied and not completely avoiding her, but they had always talked about this kind of thing. Normally, she'd have been the first one he called—before all that mess this weekend. "Is there anything I can do to help?"

"Do you have a muzzle? Or two?"

"The only one I have I'm using on Justin lately." The rhythm of their conversation was slowly resuming its normal pace. She did not want to lose this connection, regardless of what did or did not happen in the bedroom department. "It must be a 'fits-having' kind of couple of days."

"They aren't the only females giving me fits right now, either." There was another pause and another throat clearing. "Do you have time today, Claudia? I think we should talk. Face to face would be better."

Why? So he could turn down her cake offer to her face? Not going to happen if she could help it. The build-out on Decadence could wait until this all quietly faded away. "Uh, no. I don't think I have time at all today, and probably not for the next week or so. But we should definitely set up a time to go over the plans. Or you can meet with Zoe another day. I'm sure she can handle it all without a problem." Her pulse was frantic, her heart bumping into her breastbone to the point she was afraid it would be on the table any minute now.

"Now who's avoiding?"

"I am," she said and hung up before he could say another word.

Of course that wasn't the end of it, and Claudia knew it. The other shoe would drop at some point. In the meantime, she had a shop to run.

Downstairs, Claudia opened a new box of supplies that had arrived that morning, poking around inside to see what kind of fun new cake decorators had come her way. Nothing but those Styrofoam peanuts, yet, but she had hope her new professional-grade rind grater was somewhere in all the packing material.

Zoe slouched against the counter. She kept peeking out into the front of the store as if expecting something, or someone, to come through the door. She swiped her hair off her forehead and blew out a breath. "I really think that someone else should handle the lawyer thing. I don't know what Uncle Al was thinking, but if he won't deal with me, then I'm not dealing with Dex."

"Well, that sucks for you. You're the only one who has time to do this right now, and we want to make sure we have all our ducks in a row before we move forward with making May a partner. I don't want our butts hanging out in the wind with legalities." She knew the grater was in here somewhere. Why did they always have to pack everything like the deliveryman was going to drop-kick it through her door?

"Right. You're so busy, what with avoiding Nate now that you've finally figured out that he is super sexy. I heard Justin caught you all over each other. I hope you're not planning to break in the living room floor, since I think that's already been done."

Claudia looked up quickly to find Zoe with a smug smile on her face. "I don't even want to know what it is you're alluding to. I'm trying to find my grater, and I can't be distracted by your dirty birdy mind."

Zoe nudged her shoulder, dipped her hand into the white peanuts, and came out with the grater. "Oh, come on. Like you've thought completely pure thoughts since you decided to run out and grab you a piece of Nate." She handed the shiny new device over to Claudia, who hummed long and low at the back of her throat.

The hum could have been for the grater or for thoughts of Nate, but she wasn't going to tell Zoe which one. She'd simply avoid that particular conversation all together. "So how about this new guy from Sunday night?"

Zoe was obviously willing to be distracted back to her own life. "He definitely has stallion potential. I could try this one on for size without a single problem."

"Stallion or not, is he a nice guy?"

"Yeah, well, I guess so."

It was on the tip of her tongue to caution Zoe against just having fling after fling. But who was she to tell anyone how to run her love life? Claudia had enough of her own problems trying to forget that Nate had seen her as a woman for about ten glorious minutes and now he wanted to "talk." She hated talking when she knew it wasn't going to go in her favor. And this conversation could quite possibly embarrass the hell out of her.

Clearing her throat, Claudia dove back into the box of peanuts, looking for the icing tip she'd also ordered. She found the packing receipt but nothing else. The receipt showed it had been shipped, but after sifting her hands through all the packing material, she found nothing. "Can you stick your magic hand in here again and find my decorating tip?"

Zoe did as Claudia asked and came up seconds later with the wrapped plastic in her hand. She handed that over, too, then smiled. "Here you go. I don't know why you can't find these things."

"Yeah, me either."

"Perhaps you're a little blind."

"Not yet."

"Well, I can tell you a spot where you are blind."

"I do not want to have this conversation, ever, and especially not right now." The glint in Zoe's eyes did not bode well for Claudia, though. She'd been on her to call Nate about the cake thing again, and Claudia wasn't going to do it. He'd had his chance. She was not looking to be shot down again.

"You should wear something sexy when Nate comes to pick up Justin for that father-son dinner. I bet he'd change his mind in a second if you showed him what he's missing."

"Don't you have something else to do? We've been over this before. He's not interested. We'll leave it at that. His grandma is having issues, his mom is calling him day and night, and starting something between us would only end up in disaster. I'd rather have my friendship back on an even keel than have my lust satisfied."

"You were all about the cake just a few days ago." Zoe twiddled with the trailing vine on top of the cake display counter. "I think you were on the right track then."

"Well, you think wrong." Even if she wore one of Zoe's slut dresses when Nate came to pick up Justin for the dinner, she wouldn't be wowing him. She'd only come off as desperate. Besides, it wasn't as if she could lose thirty pounds in three days and fit into Zoe's size.

Speaking of the devil, though, brought him in the door, wafting a subtle hint of the cologne she'd given him for Christmas last year. He smelled good enough to eat. Despite all her protests to the contrary, Claudia was more than prepared to dig out her spoon for a taste. She should be nervous and wary about him being here so soon after she'd hung up on him, and she was. But she also knew him well enough to be sure he wouldn't drag her off for "the talk" in front of other people or at her place of business. She decided to play it as if they hadn't talked and he hadn't tried to push the issue of her recent behavior. Most likely he would follow along with the program.

"Hey, Claude, got a minute?" Nate circled around the back of her counter and took a Styrofoam peanut from the box.

"Sure." Now that she had put her worry to the back of her mind and let her lust roar to the front, she imagined wiping the drool from the corner of her mouth. He wore black pants with a pale blue dress shirt unbuttoned at the collar. It wasn't often she got to see him in something other than jeans and T-shirts or sweatshirts, and it only served to whet her appetite for Friday, when he would be in a suit coat and tie, too. Yummy. She caught herself before she leaped at him, rode him to the rubber mat behind her counter, and had her wicked way with him. "I...um...what can I do you for? I mean, do for you?" She knew she was blushing, but she'd put it down to just having come out of the kitchen, if she had to. It wasn't true, but he wouldn't have to know.

"I wanted to check the time with you for that dinner with Justin and find out if I need to buy him anything for it. I've never been to one of these with him since he's always taken you. I don't want to do anything wrong."

It didn't tear at her nearly as much this time that she wasn't going. In fact, she'd convinced herself that the time alone would be nice, and it was just one more way for Justin and Nate to bond. Not that they needed to be any closer, since they were thick as thieves. Perhaps this is what he had wanted to talk about face to face and she had wigged out for no reason.

If she'd had any resistance to him at all, his question now would have melted everything inside her. As it was, she tried valiantly to keep herself from grabbing his ears and kissing the daylights out of him. She did, however, lean in and kiss him on the cheek.

She wasn't fool enough to pass up this perfect opportunity. She lingered for a second longer and pulled away from him slowly, meeting his eyes and holding his gaze for a full minute that felt like forever.

He put his hand on his cheek, a startled expression clouding his face. "What was that for?"

"You're a great guy. I appreciate you doing this for Justin. He's so excited, he's ready to burst at the seams. So, thanks."

"Um, sure, okay." His look went from startled to confused. He seemed to shake it off in a moment. His normal grin came back onto his lips. "So is there anything I can do for Justin? If he were a girl, I'd get him a corsage or something. Do we need to have boutonnieres? Will the other kids' dads have something special for them?"

"No, but thanks for asking. I would have supplied something if you needed it."

"Hey, I'm a working man. I can afford to take my friend out to dinner."

As he leaned back against her counter with his legs crossed at the ankles, she wanted to bite him in the worst possible way. The thought arose from the back of her mind, and she pressed her tongue to the back of her teeth to keep them closed. She had to get him moving along before she really did something outrageous. Or before that other shoe dropped and he mentioned the cake thing. "Well, thanks for stopping by. He'll be waiting for you on Friday. Don't forget to dress pretty much like what you have on plus a tie and a coat. He'll be wearing the same thing."

She turned away, dismissing him and trying to think about getting to work on an elaborate anniversary cake for a couple celebrating fifty years together. She needed something to calm her hormones.

Either he didn't know she had work to do or he thought she could afford to stand around all day and handle the sight of his burly body. She felt his presence behind her, and he hadn't shifted an inch.

"Was there something else you needed?" she asked, swiping at a couple of strands of hair that had fallen out of her ruthless ponytail. She had too much baking to do today to have nice swingy hair like Zoe. Damn him for coming in on a day she looked like death warmed over. She didn't even think a fancy dress in two days was going to make an impression on him. She was about to give up on that anyway. After the way they'd gone after each other after lunch the other day, he hadn't touched her again. It was as if nothing had happened. And it was damned disappointing.

But now he was no longer leaning casually. Instead he took her by the shoulders, gently turned her toward him, and nearly blew her socks off. Or would have, if she'd been wearing any.

"I want to be your cake," he said in answer to her old, unanswered question. Then he leaned in and kissed her square on the mouth.

****

Nate walked out of the shop, probably looking as stunned as Claudia had when he'd backed off after a brief pressure of lips on lips. He had no idea what possessed him to tell her he wanted to be her cake. He had come to the decision over the past few days that she was too important to him, their relationship was too important to him, to make any changes. He'd never successfully had a long-term relationship other than his friendship with her, and he shouldn't be messing with perfection.

But she'd looked so adorable with her hair curling around her face and her flushed skin, he'd done it before he really gave it a thought. It was supposed to be—should have been—a friendly kiss on the cheek, but he'd taken it into a whole different realm. Damn. And then he'd offered to be her damn cake. He was losing his mind, for sure.

Slamming into his truck, he cranked the engine and nearly squealed out from his parking spot. There was no reason to act like a jerk and get a speeding ticket, though. He slowed down and forced his mind to remain absolutely blank on how soft Claudia's lips had been and the way cake batter smelled on her, like the richest perfume in the world...

Not working. Damn.

And now he had to go to a meeting with his dad with a boner he could probably hang shingles with. He'd have untucked his shirt if he thought he could get away with it, but he'd been told to come dressed for business to his dad's office, and you crossed Darren West at your own peril.

He had about ten minutes until he hit the office, so he switched on the radio and tried to think about anything other than Claudia and that kiss. But, like some crazy cosmic joke, every station had some song about lips and kissing or touching. Even the hard rock station had a seventies song about licking. He flicked off the radio with more force than necessary and tore the knob right off.

His cell phone rang from the seat next to him. He wanted to ignore the constant buzzing but was afraid it might be his dad with some last-minute instructions. Glancing at the display screen before flipping the phone open, he sighed in relief when he saw it was his brother. "Hey, what's up? Are you at Dad's already?"

"No, man, I'm not. I should be there in about two minutes. I wanted to catch you before you came in, though, and let you know I saw your little act in the window of Decadence. I was thinking maybe you were doing some advertising for the shop. Or maybe you were helping her get icing off her face. Maybe she had something in her eye. Anyway, I just thought it was mighty interesting to drive by on my merry way and see that little display. Good job there, big brother." His cackle ran through the line and grated on Nate's nerves.

He didn't even bother saying goodbye, just snapped the phone closed and threw it on the seat. He'd have to beat the crap out of Logan later. Right now he had to figure out how he was going to sit across from him for a whole meeting and ignore his knowing smile and leers without taking his bait. Both his brother and their dad had been trying to get Nate together with Claudia for years. Actually, they alternated between getting them together and telling him to run on out and get laid. Although maybe their prodding was better than his mom calling to harass him about when could Grandma start on some baby booties since she wasn't going to be around forever.

He would have laid his head on the steering wheel if he wasn't hurtling through town at forty miles per hour in a twenty-five-miles-an-hour zone. The cop who always sat around the corner of Blanchard Street saw him hurtling, too. Nate's day was complete when he accepted a ticket and a warning to pay attention to what he was doing while driving even if his mind was preoccupied by kissing that pretty girl down at the wedding shop.

****

Justin slammed through the door of their upstairs apartment after school that afternoon, and Claudia braced herself for anything. She'd come upstairs to take a short breather after that kiss and the things it did to her insides. Nate had said he would see her later—and then kissed her again like he couldn't get enough, now that he'd made up his mind.

As for the slamming door, maybe someone who had seen the kiss in the window earlier had said something about it to Justin. Her mom had already called to chide her for causing a ruckus in town. So had Nate's mother, and his grandma, who was doing better if still ornery. May had called, too, to congratulate her. So much for being inconspicuous.

Fortunately or unfortunately, the kiss had nothing to do with the slamming door. Justin hit her with a curve ball.

"Hey! Did you know I'm a bastard?" Happiness radiated from his every pore. Bouncing up and down on the balls of his feet, he practically vibrated with the emotion.

Caught off guard, by both the language and the completely inappropriate glee in his eyes, Claudia took a moment to calm her pounding heart before answering. "Who said that word to you? I don't want you repeating it." She said it sternly, while inside she was seething and crumbling at the same time.

But Justin just skipped past her to reach the refrigerator and jerk the door open. Then he turned around and faced her with happiness in his eyes. "It doesn't matter who said it. What does it mean? I think I know, but I want to be sure."

Claudia had always tried to tell Justin the truth, except where it concerned everything about Peter, but she was well aware this was going to be a tough conversation to have. "Sit down, honey." She patted a cushion-covered chair that matched the dining table and waited for him to plop down. His reaction was very weird, and she didn't know whether to look for him to explode or to really assume he was as happy as he appeared to be.

She wished Zoe wasn't downstairs helping out with May right now. She could use some backup. She dragged her thoughts together and picked her words carefully. Praying she would find the right ones to explain such a hurtful word. "Justin, a bastard is one of those words that we don't say in this house. If you don't know what it means, then why are you so freaking happy?"

"Because if it's true, then I can say it all I want." His grin nearly split his face. "I have to be who I am, after all."

She wanted to thunk her head on the table. He was way too smart for her liking. He was killing her. And she was trying really hard not to laugh. How on earth did she manage to raise someone who could play her like this? And didn't it just suck to have her own words thrown back in her teeth?

He seemed to puff up his chest. Claudia felt a bubble of laughter try to escape her throat, while twisting mirth clenched in her stomach. She tried to explain as carefully as she could, without snorting or yelling at him, that it wasn't really appropriate. "A bastard," she said quietly, "technically, is a child who is born outside of a marriage. But the word doesn't mean the same thing today as it did when it was originally used. The kids who said it are probably just being mean. I'm sorry you had to go through that, but today that word is generally used as a swear word. Not in the literal sense."

"So, it's true then. I am a bastard, even if it's just technically." He tapped the top of the table, bouncing in his chair and causing the legs to screech on the gray tile. More screeching as he knocked the chair back with his knees. Standing with his hands fisted in the air, he whooped around in the kitchen like a clown capering in a circus. He was the very picture of glee and merriment.

"No, Justin," she pleaded, clenching a fist to her stomach, not sure she'd be able to hold it in much longer. She reached out her other hand to snag him on his next circuit around the table, a touch to let him know that she loved him, and he sidestepped her outstretched hand before it could make contact. She let it drop silently to settle in her lap, willing away the hurt that his avoidance caused in her heart. And the completely inappropriate feeling of laughter still sitting in her stomach. "What happened before you were born was none of your fault. Just don't listen to the other kids. And I don't want you saying it, even if it is what you are. It's not funny."

His mood changed instantly like a switch had been flipped. "You can't tell me. You're not a bastard. I am. And I say I should be proud of it." Defiance shot from him like shards of glass aimed directly at Claudia's heart.

They hit their mark. All the laughter in her belly turned to lead. She tried to temper her voice, but it still came out harsh. She shook her head. It wasn't that big a deal, but she really didn't want him running around calling himself a bastard any more than she had wanted him calling Peter a sperm donor. "Stop saying that word. I told you we don't use it in this house, and I expect you to abide by my rules." Heat rose in her cheeks and burned behind her eyes.

"You didn't abide by any rules!" he shouted. "It's all your fault. Why couldn't I have been born normal, like every other kid?" And then Justin whirled on the heel of his white tennis shoe and dashed out of the kitchen.

Without any warning, she broke. "I tried," she sobbed to the empty room. "I tried." She laid her head on her crossed arms atop the table.

And she continued to weep silently, the tension coiled in her body, while she listened to Justin stomp his way down the hall, slamming the door to his room.

After several long moments, the silence in the house was overwhelming, so she went to the refrigerator and returned to sit at the round oak table again, this time contemplating a glass of wine instead of the falling darkness, as she had before. Wondering for the thousandth time what the heck had happened to her well-ordered life. And, more importantly, what was she going to do to fix it?

"Mom," Justin yelled. "Phone's for you!"

Well, at least he was talking to her. She picked up the cordless and wished she hadn't.

"Hello, Claudia. I just wanted to make sure we were on for our weekly date tonight. You know how I don't like to miss out on the prime rib on Wednesdays."

What the hell was going on? Edward sounded like nothing had happened between them over a week ago. Didn't he remember she had dumped him and stalked out of the restaurant? That hadn't been a figment of her imagination. Had it?

"Edward, we aren't dating anymore," she said. She didn't want to be hurtful, but she also wasn't going to beat around the bush, either.

"Well, of course we are, Claudia. Just because you got into a bit of a snit before doesn't mean I'm going to let you throw away our whole relationship. Now, should I pick you up at the regular time?"

She took the phone away from her ear and stared at it, then put it back. "Um, no?"

"So, you'd rather meet me there? I'm not sure I like that, Claudia. I'd rather pick you up."

"Edward, we aren't seeing each other anymore." She figured she'd try one more time before hanging up on the lunatic.

"Oh, you were serious?"

Duh. "Um, yes, yes, I was, Edward. I think you need to move on with your life and find someone who would appreciate your special brand of caring." More like smothering, but she wasn't going to go back to that now that he sounded rational.

"Well, I'm sorry to hear that, dear. I thought we were good together." He sounded sincere.

Claudia took about a second to let her heart bleed a little for him and then moved on. "Well, good luck with life."

"You, too, Claudia." And he hung up.

That went a lot better than she had thought it would

when they started the conversation. She did not need anything new happening right now.

As if in defiance of what she wanted, Claudia's cell rang with a punk song from the '80s. Nate. Well, at least this wouldn't be a bad conversation, hopefully.

Picking up her cell phone, Claudia settled into the couch and answered the call.

"Hey, Claude. How's it going?"

Snuggling down in the cushions, Claudia rested her head back against the couch. "It's going okay except for Justin now wanting to be called Bastard Justin." She explained the afternoon to him and loved the way he laughed. "Oh, and Edward called to see if we were still going out on our weekly date."

"That's bizarre. I guess on top of the hair plugs, he also has hearing issues."

Now she was the one to laugh. "So how's it going? What have you been up to today?" Conversations with Nate had always been a highlight of her day, but now they'd have a little extra zing, like a touch of lemon in a plain vanilla cake.

"Well, you're not going to like this, but I'm going to have to cut out of the dinner with Justin. My dad has a meeting out of town on the books, one he didn't tell me about, and I'm going to have to go with him. Do you think Justin is going to be pissed? Can you take him? I won't be back until late Friday night at the earliest."

Justin wasn't going to be happy, but she could take him. And it wasn't as if Nate often went back on his promises. Not to mention he did own the company with his dad, and if they had meetings then they had meetings. "I'll take him, but maybe you could take him

187

somewhere when you get back, so it will lessen the blow a little."

"Absolutely. We'll go to a ball game or something. I promise. Hell, I'll take him to Hershey Park for the day, if it will make him happy. We're having trouble on this out-of-town build, and I have to be there to smooth over feathers. You know how my dad can be sometimes."

Yes, she did, and was very thankful that Nate had not inherited that temper. "These things happen." She wrapped a fringe from the afghan around her finger. "When did you say you were going to be back?"

"Friday night late. Do you have plans on Saturday? I just realized I never took you out to dinner for the big sale at Decadence, what with the madness going on with my grandma. We should rain-check it. Maybe have some cake as dessert."

"Definite rain check for Saturday, then. I'll look forward to it." The sly tone in his voice when he said "cake" made her every nerve tingle. But she did not want to come off as a nympho or overly easy, so she kept the rest of the conversation light. They talked for a little while longer, and Claudia felt a sense of contentment with how they were connecting. No, it wasn't great balls of lust and sparkly conversation. But it was good conversation and sharing, two things she had always valued in Nate as a friend and that she would hopefully soon value in him as a lover.

Cake tasting would begin Saturday.

****

Nate hung up with Claudia and rested back against his headboard. Maybe this would actually work, being Claudia's cake. They had a lot in common and a lot of years under their belts. It wasn't like a new relationship, he thought as he flipped channels on the TV hung on the opposite wall. It wasn't all pounding hearts and blind lust, but he'd felt a definite zing down below as he talked with her, and that was a bonus. While he wouldn't admit it to any of his buddies, he did have to acknowledge that the more he thought about his past, the more he realized he was committed to Claudia on a level he had never thought too much about.

They'd been friends for years, but on closer examination, he realized he had never let another woman in the way he did Claudia. Never took dating seriously. He'd always assumed it was because he wasn't interested in the whole family and responsibility thing, but maybe it was more than that. Maybe Claudia was his "more."

Saturday felt a world away, but the anticipation would all be worth it.

Chapter Ten

Peter could do without this pressure. He'd been here for nine days and already he was ready to go home. If only his sister would let him go without all the guilt. "May, I have to leave soon. I can't hang out here indefinitely helping with Dad's house. Most of it is cleaned out and organized. If you need anything else, I'm sure Brad could help you."

"I'm only asking for a day or two more, not your entire life. I want to try to get everything done before you go. Brad has a lot going on at work, and I'm not supposed to lift heavy stuff, since I'm pregnant. I thought you had another week of vacation. Besides, you said you wanted to spend some time with Justin before you went back home. It's only Thursday. Why don't you at least stay through the weekend?"

Yeah, and hadn't that first attempt gone well, with the boy calling him a sperm donor and Peter not having any idea what to say to the boy who looked so much like him? Four more days would not make that situation any better.

"I think maybe it's time to go."

"But you just got here." May put a hand on his arm and he couldn't find it inside him to shake her off.

"I know, but I didn't find what I wanted here."

"And what did you want?"

Looking into her eyes was too difficult. He'd

wanted... Well, somewhere in his mind he'd thought he'd be able to come back here, hook up with Claudia again, take his son under his wing, and have the life he should have had ten years ago but hadn't been smart enough to keep at that time. He had been delusional. And those delusions were shot down when Claudia would barely even look at him.

But he couldn't tell his sister that. So, instead, he said, "I just think I should get out of here. I'm not doing anyone any good."

"That's not true." May's heart was in her eyes, as it always was, and he felt bad about giving her trouble. But there was no use hanging around.

The phone rang in the living room. May gave him one more pleading look, then dove to pick up the receiver. He listened with half an ear as she said hello. Her side of the conversation made almost no sense and didn't hold his attention as he foraged in the refrigerator for something to snack on before he went to pack his bags.

When he backed out of the fridge, he bumped into something. Turning around he found a beaming May standing behind him with the cordless phone tucked against her chest.

"I have a big favor for you to do," she said breathlessly. "It's something you can't turn down."

He didn't know if he liked that phrase, or the light in her eyes. This visit hadn't gone at all the way he'd thought, and anything she added to it wouldn't make things better.

"Claudia's on the phone and she wants to talk to you." May kept the phone against her chest. "She wants you to do her a favor, and you better not say no."

That put his back up even more, but his curiosity was piqued by what Claudia could possibly want from him, someone she hadn't more than a handful of words for just days ago. But he put his hand out for the phone and tried to wait patiently while May timidly handed the phone over.

"Be nice," she whispered.

He yanked the phone out of her hand and put it up to his ear. "Hello, Claudia."

"Peter."

The line hummed with a tense silence. A silence he wasn't going to fill, since he wasn't the one who'd called.

She cleared her throat. "I have something to ask, and please really think about it before you say no."

Why did everyone assume he was some coldhearted asshole? Yeah, he'd been dumb when he was younger, but he'd learned a few things since he was eighteen and ran from the prospect of a lifetime of raising a child.

"What?" he said, a little more harshly than he'd intended.

May whacked him on the arm, and he scowled at her.

Claudia cleared her throat again, and something about the sound sparked low in his gut. She needed him. For something. What he didn't know. But he did know she needed him, and this might be his way into her good graces. Perhaps he could even win her back if he did this thing for her, whatever it was.

"I need you to do something for me."

He could list a number of things he wouldn't mind doing to that fine curvy body he'd looked at all during lunch. He'd been an idiot to walk away. "What?" He made his voice lower, gentler.

"Justin would like you to take him to a father-son dinner on Friday if you're still in the area."

"But I'm just the sperm donor." It slipped out before he could stop himself. He tried to correct his colossal mistake before she hung up on him. "I'm sorry. I'm sorry. That's not what I meant to say. Please don't hang up on me."

"And why shouldn't I? I ask you for one little thing after you made that great speech about what a mistake you made, how things should have been different. But as soon as I ask one little thing, you have a freak attack."

He could just imagine her arms crossed over that impressive chest and her lips pouting. It had been a look she'd perfected years ago.

"I'm not having a freak attack." He blew out a breath and turned away from May who looked like she wanted to take the phone from him and bop him on the head with it. "You just caught me off guard."

"So?" Her tone had turned harder, probably waiting for him to disappoint her, let her down again. He had a chance here, one he would be incredibly dumb to turn down.

"Yeah, of course I'll take him." He asked for the details, and she gave them freely. May had a piece of paper under his hand and a pen ready and waiting before he even thought to ask. After writing everything down, he thanked Claudia and told her he'd be there to pick up Justin right on time. But he couldn't help pushing just a little bit more. "How about we have dinner sometime this week? You know, while I'm here.

Catch up on old times. You can tell me all about what you've been up to the last few years."

There was another telling silence across the line. Until finally she said, "I don't think I'll have time for that right now. I have a bunch of stuff to take care of for some different events coming up." She hesitated, and he read a wealth of dismissal in that moment. "But thanks for helping out. Justin will appreciate having a male to take him to the dinner. I'll call you if I think of anything else."

And just like that, she hung up the phone. He stood with May at his elbow for a long moment before clicking off the phone in his hand.

"Thank you," she said quietly.

"Yeah, no big," he said absently. But inside he was in turmoil. What was he going to do with the child he barely knew for the unknown number of hours this dinner would last? How was he going to interact with a ten-year-old he didn't even know? He hadn't been around children since he was one himself. This might not have been his best idea, but now he was stuck, and without the prize of dinner with Claudia dangling at the end.

****

Claudia hung up the phone and leaned her head against the cabinet in the kitchen. What had she just done? She'd asked a favor of the man she'd sworn never to give even another thought. And now she felt beholden to him. When he'd mentioned dinner, it occurred to her that it might not be a bad idea for them to be on better speaking terms, if Peter was going to be a small part of Justin's life again. But she didn't want to give any of her limited time to a man she didn't want to have anything to do with. She'd much rather spend that time with Nate.

Nate, who was not available to talk to because of being out of town. He'd left this morning after giving her a kiss that would have to see her through to Saturday. Her lips were still tingling. No matter how much she wanted to pick up her cell and call him, just to hear his voice, she wouldn't lay this on him when he couldn't do anything about it. Especially since he'd felt bad enough about not taking Justin in the first place.

Claudia had offered to take Justin, since things with Nate had fallen through, but Justin had thought about it and asked for Peter.

Jeez, had that been a blow to her ego.

Or maybe it was a testament to the way she'd raised him. Either way, it appeared she wouldn't be going to this dinner and Peter would. She only hoped it would be fine, and that Peter would be the adult. Justin was smart and would know if his biological father didn't have an ounce of interest in him. Her head hurt just thinking about all the complications that could crop up on this outing, and nerves pounded behind her eyes.

Please let this work out. Justin deserved a break lately. He'd actually taken the news about Nate pretty well, even though Claudia had expected him to have some sort of complete breakdown. Hell, *she* was on the verge of some kind of complete breakdown. Now she might feel the need to go out with Peter, just to be nice to him after he'd so quickly agreed to help her out.

Zoe saved her from her own thoughts by banging in at the back door and throwing herself lengthwise on the couch. Now here was something Claudia could do and not feel useless. Because as much as it appeared

Nate wanted her, it was going to have to wait.

But Zoe's problems she could do. She'd put her cake fantasies aside for the moment and sort things out in her sister's life. Maybe then she'd feel like she was worth something.

"That bad, huh?" Claudia said, stroking Zoe's hair as she sat next to her on the couch.

Zoe groaned.

"Hey, here's something that ought to make you giggle. Apparently we're going to be hearing the term 'bastard' around here a lot over the next few days. It might even replace 'sperm donor.'"

Zoe popped her head out of the cushions. "Bastard?"

"Yep, your nephew heard from some idiotic kids that he's a bastard, and the boy has decided to take the term to heart and embrace himself."

Zoe snickered. "Sorry. But bastard?"

"Uh-huh. And he may even have convinced himself that we should call him Bastard Justin for the next little while. He likes it and thinks that because it's technically true he should be allowed to use it." Claudia smoothed Zoe's hair from her forehead. "You can laugh all you want. I was barely able to keep it in when he was talking. Although things got a little nasty at the end. Oh, and Peter is going to be taking our dear Bastard Justin to the father-son dinner. I actually had to call and ask him—and deflect his dinner invitation. So if you think you have it bad, maybe that will help you feel a little bit better."

"Nice."

"I thought you might like that." She ran a hand down Zoe's arm.

"Why are men such bast...well, I guess 'jerk' is probably the better word at this point."

Now it was Claudia's turn to snicker. "I have no idea. Maybe just to make us insane? I can't even seem to get some time to myself for Nate, either. And now he'll be gone until Saturday. My cake is not happening."

Zoe sighed. "I think I might just go on a sweets-free diet."

"I guess it really was bad."

"You have no idea. But at least you have Nate to look forward to. Say goodnight to the bastard for me."

"Will do." Claudia took a glass of wine out onto the deck and just sat for a little while, daydreaming in the dark to keep herself from dwelling too much on all that could go wrong tomorrow night at the dinner for Justin's school.

****

Nate fidgeted in his car the whole way home on Friday. He'd wrapped up things as early as he could, working through the whole night Thursday to get on the road early enough to try and make the father-son dinner. He'd brought a suit with him for meetings and had it cleaned this afternoon when the meetings were over, then dressed in it so he could go straight to the elementary school's gymnasium and hopefully surprise Justin and let Claudia off the hook as the boy's date for another year.

It had killed him to tell the kid he couldn't make it to the dinner. But he hadn't wanted to make promises, in case things didn't go as planned and he didn't make it back in time. Nate was huge on keeping his promises.

Plus, this way he got to see Claudia in a dress.

God, he hoped she was wearing a pair of her killer heels. Nothing was like seeing her long calves pumped up by a pair of spike heels.

And there he went again, fantasizing about her. It was as if, ever since she'd kissed him, some kind of floodgate had opened and he could view everything about her over the years through a new set of eyes.

He wasn't dumb. He'd always known she was a female. But he'd just never seen her as a woman until she'd laid her lips on his and damn near made his toes curl.

He wanted to get back to her as much as he wanted to get to Justin, but in a different way, obviously. He was really hoping, though, that he could finish up the dinner with Justin and then finish out the evening with Claudia, fulfilling those promises she'd made with her eyes and her lips and her hands.

He pressed down on the accelerator a little harder, drove a little faster, to get to her and to Justin. Whipping into the school's parking lot, he snagged a lucky parking spot near the front. Damn traffic had made him over an hour late. He'd only get to eat dessert with his guy now. But at least it was something.

He straightened his tie and patted down his hair while hustling to the side doors of the gym. He'd have one more hour with Justin, and then he could go home to Claudia and see if they could find a little time together. He was ready and raring for that time together.

The rumble of a hundred men and boys greeted him when he yanked the door open. He stepped in and let it all wash over him. He'd never been invited to this event before, and it had meant the world to him that

Justin had made the invitation. And now he was going to try to fulfill it for his guy the best he could.

Everyone was seated except for a few people picking at what food was left at the buffet. He looked around, trying to spot the one woman in the crowd. He was baffled to not find her sitting at one of the round tables. Maybe they hadn't come at all. That made him feel even worse.

He pulled his cell phone out of his pocket and was ready to dial Claudia to find out what had happened when he spotted Justin sitting next to an older gentleman. Nate had no idea who the man was, or why he would have brought Justin. But then he looked to the left and couldn't believe his eyes. For there sat Peter, large as life, in the seat that should have been Nate's.

It took a second to reconcile the picture with his brain. Where the hell was Claudia? And why on earth was Peter sitting there in a suit and tie—and talking to the guy next to him instead of to Justin? It just didn't compute.

But then it did. Maybe Peter was trying to take a bigger part in his son's life—because, even though Nate had never really thought of Peter as Justin's father, in actuality he was. They had the same blood running through their veins, even if Peter had barely acknowledged it in over ten years. But this couldn't be a bad thing, for Justin and Peter to bond a little.

If Nate felt any kind of jealousy rising, he soon squashed it. The kid knew who he wanted to hang out with, and Nate hadn't been able to make the dinner. Maybe Claudia had been busy, too, since she'd thought she'd have a night to herself. That left Peter, who just happened to be in town. Made sense to him.

With that thought in mind, then, he didn't want to ruin what could be the beginning of a new relationship. He started creeping backward, hoping no one would notice him as he made a discreet exit.

He'd almost made it to the double doors when Justin's head jerked up like a wolf scenting prey. His eyes zeroed in on Nate, and the slight frown on his young face turned into a full-fledged smile of relief. That couldn't be good.

The boy was up and out of his chair before Nate could blink. Peter spared him a quick glance before returning to his conversation with the man next to him. That didn't look good, either.

And then Nate's arms were filled with boy. His heart was just filled, period.

"Oh, Nate, thanks so much for coming. You don't know how terrible it's been." When Justin stepped back from burying his face in Nate's chest, he looked close to tears. That was saying something for his guy.

"What's up?"

Justin blew out a sigh that ruffled Nate's tie. "I don't want to talk about it right now." He turned pleading eyes on Nate, the ones Nate had never learned to resist. "Can you please, please, get me out of here?"

"Whoa, whoa, whoa." Nate put a hand under Justin's chin and looked into his troubled face. "What's this about getting out of here? Don't you still have an hour left before the dinner thing is done?"

"I can't stay here. Please take me home."

"But what about Peter?" Nate put his arm around Justin, but he wasn't budging until he figured out what was going on.

"Peter is a jackass." Justin flushed and bit his lip.

"I'm not going to call you on the language, but I'm going to need more than that, if you think I'm going to break you out of this joint."

Justin slipped his hand into Nate's and gave him a squeeze. "He doesn't have the faintest clue."

"That might be true, but what are we supposed to tell him and your mom about you leaving with me?"

Justin clasped his hands in front of his chest. "Please!"

"It's that important?" Nate didn't feel good about stepping in where he wasn't wanted, but he could clearly remember what an ass Peter had been when they were in high school. From what he'd seen, the guy hadn't changed much. This must have been torture for Justin.

"It's really that important." The sincerity in Justin's voice was no joke.

"Wait here. I'll go see what I can do." He left Justin standing at the double doors and tried to figure out what the hell he was going to say to Peter. What if the man didn't realize Justin was having a horrible time?

But he didn't have to worry so much. As soon as he approached Peter and the other man looked up, the relief in Peter's eyes was crystal clear. "Please, man, tell me you've come to save me. I don't have the faintest damn idea what I'm doing here. All these fathers know their kids' batting average."

Nate knew Justin's. It was .178.

"They know his favorite color and what his favorite food is."

Green. And Tastykakes, when he could get away with it, via Nate. Claudia wouldn't let him near that over-processed treat. But Nate didn't say any of these things, because Peter did truly look bewildered. Nate knew how tough this must have been for both the kid and the man. He wouldn't say "father," since all these things would be common knowledge for anyone interested in a child's life. But Peter had never even met Justin until this week. Had no contact with him at all other than one birthday card when he was three.

"Justin was thinking I could drive him home, since I'm here," Nate said, looking down at the carpet and giving the guy the chance to gracefully bow out of the whole thing.

Peter took it. "That would be great, man. If you don't mind, I'll head back to May's. I have some packing to do. I think Justin was done here, anyway. I'll just say goodbye on my way out." He clapped Nate on the shoulder as he walked toward the double doors.

It was that easy. Nate hung back for a second to let father and son say goodbye to each other. The body language was all wrong. Justin leaned away from Peter when the man put an arm over his shoulders. Peter seemed to take the hint and offered his hand for a more manly shake. Then he was out the door.

Taking his time, Nate strolled over to Justin and offered him the one thing he probably needed the most. "Ice cream?"

The kid's whole face creased into a smile. "Yeah."

****

Peter slammed a hand into his steering wheel as he tore out of the elementary school parking lot. The Mustang rumbled under him and classic Depeche Mode shot from the speakers, drowning out the voices mocking him in his head.

He'd failed tonight, there were no two ways about it. He didn't know the first thing about the strange alien person who carried his blood. While other fathers were whipping out baseball trading cards of their kids and talking about all the activities and sports they participated in, he was hard pressed to remember what Justin's middle name was. He had no idea if Justin played sports at all. He couldn't even come up with whether he liked chicken or beef at dinner.

The whole night had been a disaster, beginning with the moment he'd picked the boy up and seen how stunning Claudia looked in a pair of sweats with thick, brightly striped socks on her feet.

He didn't know what the hell he was doing here, or why he had come back, other than to help his father. He wasn't being much help there, either. He and Roger had never really gotten along. His father liked to brag about the business Peter did and the deals he made, but they never talked like May and Roger talked.

This visit was no exception. Normally, his family came to him. May had tried for a while, once she came back home, to get him to take an interest in Justin. She'd sent kindergarten pictures and drawings the boy had done. But Peter had had no interest. He had more deals to put together, his own life to lead. When he'd left Claudia three months pregnant and pursued his dreams, he'd never meant to come back.

And he'd been right to do so. There was nothing here for him. He should just go home now.

He went back to May's, told her his decision, listened to her bitch about it, and then went to bed to get some sleep before his start out of town the next morning. He'd made his decision, and he would not be swayed.

He only had one more thing to do on his way out of town.

****

Claudia's cell phone rang in her Decadence apron pocket a half hour before a bride was scheduled to come in for a cake taste-test. She did not have time for this, but she had been expecting a call from the principal at Justin's school to discuss thoughts on how to get him to stop asking the other children to call him Bastard Justin. Normally the principal didn't make calls outside of school hours, but Claudia had made the man and his wife their anniversary cake six months ago, and he now professed to be in love with her, or at least with her baking skills. Maybe she could use some of her baking points to get the principal to go easy on Justin about the language and the punishment for it.

She answered, though she did not recognize the number, and then she wanted to hang up immediately. She did not have the time or the inclination to deal with Peter today, of all days. She and Nate were finally going to test a little cake and icing of their own tonight, with Justin at her mom's and Zoe out of town for the evening. He would not ruin that for her.

"What can I do for you?" she asked after he had said hello but then nothing else. The silence hung in the space between them uncomfortably as she braced herself for nearly anything.

He cleared his throat, and her stomach heaved a little. Clearing his throat had always meant he was about to tell her something she would not like.

"I was going to stop by to see you."

"I'm really busy today, Peter." May had told her

how he had been asking questions, trying to get to know her and Justin through his sister, but May had turned him down and told him to do it himself if it was important to him. So far that had not happened, so it must not have been important. Fine with her.

"I said I was going to stop by, but I decided against it. I am actually at a rest stop about an hour away, on my way home." He rushed on before she could say anything. "After that dinner with Justin, I realized that I'm not needed here. I'm not even welcome here. I should have stayed away altogether."

Part of her wanted to feel bad for him, but in all honesty he had made the decisions that had led to this moment, and she wasn't to blame. Still, she couldn't let him think he wasn't welcome at his sister's home, no matter how it had thrown her into a tailspin to have him in the same town again. "I'm sure you're welcome if you choose to come back sometime. May loves having you here."

He chuckled, but it was a sad sound. "I know you're not that obtuse. I'm fully aware that May loves having me here. My dad and I, however, get along better when we're not in the same state, and you and I are never going to go back to what we were."

"No, Peter, we're not."

"I really thought, on the way here over a week ago, that I would be able to come back and claim what should have been mine all along, what I walked away from. I was dumb to think it would be that easy."

"Not dumb, just maybe arrogant or naïve."

"Thanks. I think."

Now she chuckled, but it was just as sad. "You gave me something really precious all those years ago, and there will always be a little part of you with me in Justin. In the way his eyes look just like yours and the way he throws himself into things."

"But he doesn't need me, and neither do you."

It was a stark and frank insight from Peter, who had rarely looked outside himself and what he wanted. "I'm sorry."

"Don't be. You made a life for yourself and for Justin in a way that I never could have. He knows he's loved, and even if it's not blood, he has a father."

"Peter…"

"No, Claude, I saw the way he ran to Nate. The man was all Justin could talk about at that dinner. How he plays baseball with him and they have mock fights and trounce each other on video games. He takes him to pizza and tells him to treat you right. He gives it to him straight and expects him to be his best person while he's showing him how, Justin said. He looks up to Nate and wants to be like him someday. What else is a father, if not a role model who loves you for you but wants you to be your best, better than the father is?"

"I…" Claudia had never heard him talk like this.

"Anyway, I just wanted to tell you, because I didn't want you to think I was leaving like I did last time."

Last time, when he had left without a word, begging his father to let her know he had gone to move into his dorm room early, to get ready for his fall classes.

"And I'm not going to be back for a while. May's pissed, but she'll have to get over it. I'm sure she'll send me pictures galore of the baby when it's born, and it will be good enough for me if not for her. It's all I can offer." He took a breath. "Speaking of pictures, if you want to send one or two of Justin over the years, I wouldn't mind. One of those baseball trading cards everyone was talking about. And maybe some of the things he's drawing, too. He drew me a cartoon on a napkin at the dinner, and it was pretty good. If he ever wants to pursue something like that, give me a holler and I'll be happy to shell out some money to help him get into a good college."

She was going to get a word into this conversation if she had to yell it. "Peter, I appreciate the offer, and I will send you some pictures, but you don't have to cut yourself off completely just because things didn't fall into place the first time you tried. Justin could possibly warm up to you if you spent more time with him, and May is going to be far more than pissed if you don't come see her baby before she can travel." What was she saying? She could be free of him indefinitely, and here she was inviting him to come back in a matter of months.

"You always did have a bigger heart than me, Claudia. I'll see, when the time comes. But for now, I think you ought to run down Nate and officially make him a dad to that boy. He's done all the work and been by your side for years. He had a thing for you when we were together, and he threatened to beat the shit out of me if I ever hurt you. And then he did when I left for college. He came and gave me a shiner I didn't get rid of for days. He loves you in a way I never would have been good at. Patiently, quietly, wholly."

More insight, and this was much weightier. Nate loved her, in Peter's eyes? Nate had punched Peter? She'd have to wrap her head around that later.

"I'm going to go now," he said, cutting into her

reeling thoughts. "I have to get back home and you have to get on with your life. Thanks for raising a great kid, Claude. You did it right all by yourself, and though it probably means nothing, I'm proud of you." He hung up, leaving her to sputter. But she couldn't sputter long, because she had that cake test-tasting in less than five minutes.

Still, she found May and asked her to greet the bride when she came in and let her know Claudia would be out in just a moment. Claudia needed a moment to breathe and think through what had just happened before she put her happy face on and handed out sweets.

Back in the small office with its more comfortable new chairs, she sat and hung her head down near her knees. Talking with Peter had been shades of the man she had fallen in love with when they were teenagers. The one who would talk with her for hours while holding her hand and staring at the stars. To say he broke her heart when he left was a lie, since he had broken it two months prior when he offered to pay for her abortion because he wasn't ready to be a father. He couldn't see how he could go to college and get a degree when he'd have diapers to change and a squalling kid to deal with. He'd changed in that moment into someone she was better off without. She knew now it had probably just been his panic talking, but it really had turned out better for all of them that he had been able to walk away.

She cried, because she could, for the first time in a long time. She felt free from the past, in the present, and for the future.

Chapter Eleven

After wiping her eyes and doing her best to repair herself, Claudia walked out to the front of Decadence, zeroing in on Nate, right outside the front window, adjusting that tool belt that made her mouth water and her legs quiver. He raised a hand and smiled at her just as the front door opened and the bride came in with her mother in tow.

The timing could be better, but Claudia's first duty was to her work right now. Nate—and fantasies about him—would just have to wait a little while longer. She had cake tasting of her own to look forward to, and the freedom to truly enjoy it without the threat of Peter hanging over her head any longer. She hadn't realized how much his presence in town had weighed on her and how much she had feared he would want visitation rights. The thought of sharing her son with his father when she'd never had to do that before had ridden her like a nightmare. But now it was gone.

"Good afternoon, ladies," Claudia said as she took a hand of each. "It's so good to see you again." This was another bride who had been here with all of her female relatives a few short weeks ago. She had been in for flowers since then, but the cake decision had been put off for a while longer. With the wedding only weeks away, Claudia should have been frantically calling her to reschedule, but honestly, with all the turmoil recently she had forgotten until an e-mail from the bride came in this morning, requesting the meeting.

"I just love this place," Penny Plinks said, twirling round in a circle for a second. She was at least forty even if she was acting like one of those teenage girls the ten-year-old Claudia had followed around looking for tidbits about boys all those years ago.

"We're glad you do, Penny," Claudia said. "We've really enjoyed working with you for this special event. You're going to be stunning in your dress." Claudia's smile was genuine, but it widened when she caught Nate waving at her from the front window. She discreetly flicked her fingers at him behind her back and then returned her attention to the people in front of her.

Leading them over to a small café table, Claudia seated both ladies on tall, cushy chairs, then brought out seven plates, each with a different cake she had made this morning.

"I shouldn't eat too much." The bride, Penny, eyed the cake plates like a cat after the canary.

"Oh, these samples are calorie-free," Claudia said, smiling at the nervous woman. "May and I have an agreement that any cake tasted in here doesn't go anywhere near hips or butts. It's forbidden."

Picking up the fork, Penny hovered the utensil over each individual plate while licking her lips. "Before I try it, I have a question."

"Hopefully I have an answer." Claudia smiled at the mom and then the bride, while inside she braced herself for a request for a cake shaped like a particular continent or an outline of the bride and groom. Both had happened in the past and were more of a challenge than an inconvenience.

"Do you have anything with sprinkles?"

Claudia had heard stranger questions but couldn't name any at the moment. "I could add sprinkles, if you want. May I ask why?"

"Oh, Penny, I thought we had discussed this. A proper wedding cake does not have sprinkles, my dear." Betty Plinks patted Penny's hand and turned to Claudia. "She has this thing about sprinkles. It's lovely but silly."

"I'd be interested in hearing it." Claudia smiled. "We like to know our clients and what's important to them for their special day."

"Thank you, Claudia. You came very highly recommended by a friend. And that's one of the reasons I insisted we come to you. Your attention to detail." She turned to Betty. "And it's not silly, Mother, it's true." Penny, her brown hair shining and her lightly lined face glowing, faced Claudia, her hands clasped at her chest. "I want sprinkles because they symbolize the way I feel about my Matt. I was a plain cake kind of girl for so many years, and then he walked in the door at my parents' hardware store and introduced me to sprinkles."

Her brown eyes had gone dreamy, and Claudia waited for the gushing to start about how strong he was and the broad shoulders that made her melt, or the fact her biological clock was winding down and he had come just in time. But Penny surprised her. "He took me from plain cake straight past the icing and on to the sprinkles. He makes me smile and laugh and puts that little extra something in my life I'd thought I could live without."

"That's lovely," Claudia said, thinking she had been that kind of woman one day a long, long time ago. She'd never thought of the special moments with someone as sprinkles, but at some point she'd started settling for stale cookies. Now she wanted cake with Nate. Just cake by itself was good. After all, not everyone could stand the sprinkles, and some people even scraped the icing off the cake before eating it. Both could be too much to handle.

Penny tittered nervously after her mini-trip down lovers' lane, and Betty just smiled. "We're so excited you could fit us in." She took a forkful of the marble cake and nibbled at it.

"It's my pleasure, Mrs. Plinks. I wouldn't miss working for this wedding for the world. We appreciate you coming in."

Betty waved an obscenely jeweled hand. "Pshaw! We wouldn't even think of going anywhere else."

Thank God, Claudia couldn't help but think. They'd been working hard for years to build their reputation. And the boost to her personal confidence was very welcome, especially after the debacles of the last couple of weeks.

The conversation moved away from sprinkles and on to the plates of cake. Claudia detailed the types and the icings that would best complement, but through it all she couldn't stop thinking about Nate. Was he sprinkles? Was he more than just cake? Was she cheating herself by thinking she would be happy with only cake? As much as she didn't want stale cookies, perhaps she was looking for more. He did all the things Penny seemed to think were sprinkles. His attention to Justin, to her, the way he made her feel tingly with just a glance, the care he took with her and her son. The way he had always been around and never made it seem as if they were infringing on his time. Maybe all along she had already had her cake sitting on the plate in front of her without taking a nibble until Nate had rocked her carefully managed world with his kiss.

After four more samples, Betty gripped Claudia's hands like a vise and, despite the pain, Claudia kept a smile on her face. The sheen of tears in Claudia's eyes probably passed for happiness, but her only concern was a brief foray into the little she knew about blood and how long it would continue circling in her hands before they started to tingle from the woman's death grip. They chose the Double Deluxe Chocolate Fantasy with Butter Cream Icing, just as Claudia had known they would.

"Thank you, thank you," the matronly Betty said, sniffing into her lace handkerchief. "You don't understand how much this means to us."

Claudia could just imagine. The bride-to-be was forty if she was a day and had confided in Claudia that this was her first wedding. May had taken special pains to create a dress that would flatter the plump woman and make her feel fifteen—well, maybe five—years younger. Claudia had made it a point to get as much information as she could regarding her likes and dislikes. This would probably be the only wedding for the younger Ms. Plinks, and Claudia, May, and Zoe wanted to make sure it was really special. "It was my pleasure, Mrs. Plinks. Thank you for allowing us to be a part of Penny's wedding."

Claudia stretched her face into a full-fledged smile regardless of the continuing pain in her hands. She was going to have to deal with those damn prickly tingles once the woman let go, and she wasn't looking forward to it.

The second they walked out the front door, Claudia vigorously rubbed her hands together to get the needle-like sensation to fade. She watched Nate walk up to Penny and hug her, and she was reminded that he had been the friend who recommended that Penny come to see her and Decadence if she really wanted to have all her dreams for her perfect wedding happen. Penny wiped something from her eye as she stood back and held onto Nate's arms. She said something, and they both turned to where Claudia stood in the window shamelessly taking the scene in. Penny waved, gave Nate another hug, and left.

She and Nate stared at each other through the big pane of glass. He was backed by a blue sky and the trees across the road. It was a normal, everyday sight, and yet it set her heart racing. It wasn't some romance novel cover, it wasn't even romantic in the least, except that it was Nate, the fulfillment of every one of her needs and desires, if she would admit that he was the sprinkles. Not just cake, not just icing, not just a body to satisfy her desires or a shoulder to lean on when times were tough. Not just a best friend who had stuck by her all these years.

He was her helpmate, someone who believed in her when she didn't believe in herself. Someone she did the same for and would continuously over the years. He was someone she wanted to grow old with, not just as besties with different paths that would lead them back to each other over and over again through the years. She didn't want him to belong to anyone but her.

The breath backed up in her lungs, and she felt lightheaded. She was going to change all the rules to a game that hadn't even really started yet. She was going to tell him what she wanted and let him tell her he wanted the same.

That thought made her feel a little sick in the stomach. She sought out the chair where the happy bride had recently sat tasting cake for her wedding day. She had been so happy and so sure in what she was doing. Knew that Matt was it for her for the rest of her life.

But Claudia had thought the same thing long ago. Long enough that she knew things like that didn't always last, no matter how much you wanted them to. Life would have been much different and less rich if Peter had stuck around, she knew that. She also knew what it felt like to be abandoned and never wanted to experience it again.

"Emergency girl meeting!" she yelled, startling the only customer in the building. Mrs. Beecher gave her a smile.

"I know all about those girl meetings, and I hope this one is about that yummy hunk outside, dear. I heard you were kissing him and thought it was about darn time that you got a clue. Go get him!"

When Mrs. Beecher patted her arm affectionately and told her she'd be back after lunch to continue shopping, Claudia gave her a weak smile. It was all she could manage as she headed for the small back office with its new comfy chairs. It was last on the list for expansion. Nate was going to build out the office into the back yard to allow for them to have three desks, bookshelves, and filing cabinets. She'd miss the coziness of this current room, probably, but not right now as she tried to pace and found it frustrating to have to wind around the bigger chairs and the desk, all arranged tightly in the small space.

May and Zoe showed up within seconds and took a seat. They both brought their feet up off the floor and sat in the Criss-Cross-Applesauce position to avoid Claudia's strides.

When Claudia looked over at them, they were both smiling at her smugly.

"What?" she said, standing still for a moment.

"Penny told you her sprinkles story," May said first, with a smirk that turned into a huge smile.

"Um, yes." How did she know that?

"She told me the same story when I was making her dress, and I told her to come in and make sure she told you, since Zoe had already made the cake announcement after hearing Penny's sprinkles story, too."

Zoe's smile was even bigger, if possible. It looked like she would split her face in half at any moment. Looking at May, she said, "I told you that would get to her!"

Claudia started sputtering. Once she regained control of her tongue, she just stood there with her mouth open.

"The carp impression is not doing you any more favors than it did me the other day." Zoe let her feet rest back on the floor. "You were ripe to finally see Nate as something more than a friend. I've been waiting forever for you to get with him. My fifteen-year-old heart went pitty-pat every time he held Justin, and I knew he was the one for you even then."

"I didn't see it that early, Claudia," May confided. "I was still hoping you would get back together with my brother, but once I heard the sprinkles story and you told me about Nate being your cake, I knew it was going to work out for you. It's one of the reasons I told Peter to back off before he took himself back to Ohio."

"But, I…"

Zoe cut in. "That's why Mom hasn't been introducing you to any more of those supposedly eligible bachelors. She never meant for you to actually get involved with them, because she kept hoping you would see Nate differently."

"So, you…"

"Conspiracy!" Zoe yelled. "I love conspiracies that work out right!"

May laughed, but Claudia gave Zoe the evil eye even as she smiled. "Just you wait until it's your turn."

"Eh, I'm not worried, and neither is May, since she's already married." Zoe shrugged. "I'm not falling, but it's been such a pleasure watching you realize what was right in front of you from day one."

"So, do we still have an emergency?' May asked, rising from her chair. "Because I have a dress order that needs to be done this, and I have an ultrasound scheduled for this afternoon."

"How exciting!" Zoe said, far overusing her limit of acceptable exclamation points for the day.

Claudia used one of her own. "Yes, we still have an emergency!"

"How do you figure?" Zoe asked, looking honestly perplexed. May joined her in the look, and they resembled a pair of bookends. Did they seriously not see how this would change her whole life and her plan?

The potential hazards of not just cake but sprinkles? Of putting faith in the whole sprinkles thing? In her possibly moving toward marriage and a true shared relationship for the very first time in her entire life?

"I am scared shitless."

That was all it took for both of the other women to crowd around her and say soothing things. But it was Zoe who finally stepped back and took Claudia's chin in her hand. "You can do this. You have chosen the one man in the world that I trust your happiness to completely. Now don't screw it up."

She and May shoved her out of the office before she was ready and then continued on with the shoving, straight out the door. Once on the sidewalk, Claudia looked at Nate, really looked at him in profile as he was checking the measurement of a window.

His hands were solid and big; his heart was the same. He had been with her through everything, every milestone, every setback, every hurdle, every triumph. And she wanted him, heart, mind, and body, more than she had ever wanted anyone.

She strode purposefully over to him and tapped his shoulder. He turned toward her with a smile and a hello on his lips that she promptly took into her mouth.

This was no exploratory kiss, it wasn't one that was testing or teasing. This was her pouring her soul into him, and him breathing his back into her.

****

Nate broke contact with Claudia, feeling as if his world had just spun off its axis, been jerked back, and now was turning the opposite way.

"I love you," Claudia said before he could catch his breath. "I love you and I want everything. I want the

218

cake, I want the icing, I want sprinkles and cake toppers, sugar flowers, plastic ribbon, those fake confection sugar things you can buy at the grocery store. I want all of you. And I want you to have all of me."

"Claudia…"

But he was cut off by a shrill whistle from over his left shoulder. "All right, bro!" Logan called out from the ladder to the second floor. "Finally going to reel in the one you never actually fished for. Long damn time coming, man! But it should be that much better, right?"

Nate very deliberately went to the ladder and shook the bottom just enough to scare his younger brother.

"Okay, okay. Man," he said, but he was smiling, and so was Claudia.

"I know I should have waited for tonight, or at least somewhere more private, but I wanted you to know as soon as I did. I love you. I'm hoping that was what you were going to say, back before your rude brother interrupted us." She shook the ladder a little harder, hard enough for Logan to hold onto the window sill of the second floor, just in case.

Taking her hands in his, he looked into the eyes he had seen change time and time again, from flashing with anger to drowning in sorrow. From loving and kind to hurt and distraught. And through all of it she had been his Claudia, no matter how many times he had tried to pretend otherwise. "I love you with all I have, Claude, and I always have."

"What the hell took you so long to say anything then, you big bozo? You could have saved me a bunch of stupid dates, not to mention those awful flats that I will never wear again, if you'd just spoken up."

"See you got yourself a live one," Fred called out as he helped his girlfriend out of the car across the street. Now they had even more witnesses. Great.

"What are you doing over here?" Nate loosely held Claudia's hand while he got a good look at the woman who had snagged his neighbor's heart. Big pinkish hair dominated a petite, rounded woman. Glasses perched on her small nose and only slightly dimmed the vibrant twinkle in her faded eyes.

"Edna wants to do a little decadent shopping, since I told her we should get hitched, and I can't say no to my loveykins, can I?"

"You did not tell me, Fred Watson." She turned to Nate while smacking Fred in the arm with her purse. "He got down on one knee and asked for my hand in marriage. He said he wants to grow old together, the silly thing. I told him I'd grow old*er* with him but I was already old."

Fred's big laugh was accompanied by her tinkling laughter, and it was beautiful.

"Now, son," Fred said. "I have some business to attend to with this young lady there in your arms, but we can do the flower thing first, if you need to take a little time." Fred waggled his eyebrows.

But there was no way Nate was going to drag her upstairs and have his way with her, frantically, when Justin would be home in less than an hour, by his watch, and Logan was in the window, and Fred was downstairs. Talk about witnesses.

"I'm going to walk Claudia around the block, and then she'll be right back with you."

"Take your time there, son. It'll give me more time to make eyes at Edna and talk her into trying a few things on for me out of Ms. May's collection."

"Take a lesson from that man," Claudia whispered in his ear.

"Yeah, take a lesson from me and get that girl around the corner where you can kiss her senseless without all these eyes watching." Fred laughed and Claudia blushed.

"We're going."

Nate had taken three steps with Claudia's hand in his when Fred's next words stopped him in his tracks. "Always thought that girl was made for him. Circled each other for years, but they have that kind of time. You, my dear Edna, were smart enough to talk me into things much sooner."

And then Fred was in Decadence and Claudia and Nate stared at each other on the front sidewalk.

"Let's go to the park."

Nate eyed her short black dress and the way it hugged her every curve. The benches were mostly clean at the park, but she might regret her decision. If she needed to do this out there, though, who was he to complain?

He led her through the concrete entryway and waited for her to take a seat on the wooden bench under an oak tree. She continued to stand and pace.

"You go ahead and have a seat. I need to stand for this. I'm too agitated to sit."

He did as she asked, wanting to make sure she wasn't going to bolt.

"I'm hoping you heard every word I said and believe them all. I heard about sprinkles today, and it changed things for me."

"I've known you loved me. But aren't I just the

cake? What is the significance of sprinkles?" He braced himself for the answer. He wanted to be the sprinkles, whatever it meant. He wanted that badly.

"No!" She yanked at her hair, pulling the pins out of her beautifully arranged waves. "God, how stupid am I?"

He didn't think he was supposed to answer that question, under penalty of death.

"I mean every word and regret every moment I haven't recognized you as more than Nate-my-friend."

"I've liked being Nate-your-friend, though. Maybe it just wasn't time for us."

"I think it's time for us now," she said.

"This doesn't have anything with Peter leaving, does it? I don't want you to settle because you're panicked." Though it was one of the hardest things he'd ever had to say, there was no way he was going into this with his eyes clouded. Though it was many years since she and Peter had last been together, he was her last significant relationship and Nate did not want to be the rebound.

"There is no Peter. He just wanted to see if he could get a ready-made family without any of the work. Without any of the work you've done all these years without me even realizing it."

"Oh no." He held up his hands. "You've done all the work with Justin. He loves you and is a great kid because of you."

"And because of you. You always have been there for him and for me."

"So I'm the sprinkles?" He was almost afraid to ask in case his hearing had been faulty earlier.

"I don't know if I'd call you sprinkles, actually."

He felt his face fall into a frown. Why couldn't he be her sprinkles? "I want to be the sprinkles."

"No, Nate, what I need is the sugar."

"Huh?"

She came and sat on his thighs, snuggling into him as if his lap had been made for her. And maybe it was.

"Sugar is the base for the cake, for the icing, for the sprinkles. It's the thing you need for all of it to come together. I'd call you the eggs, since that's the binding ingredient and I want to be bound to you, but I don't think that's nearly as romantic, and it doesn't sound as good as calling you my sugar."

"Does this mean I'm going to fatten you up?" he joked, squeezing her and wanting to kiss her until neither of them could breath.

"Only if you plan on getting me pregnant."

His breath backed up in his lungs. "Do you want that?" God, to watch Claudia grow big again, this time knowing it was *his* child living and kicking inside her. Rubbing her belly again, knowing it was his son or daughter rolling inside her womb. Talking to the baby and loving it as much as he loved the son she already had.

"I want it all, Nate, and I want it with you."

"What about Justin?"

"Are you kidding? Justin is going to be over the moon. He's going to be home soon, so if you're planning on kissing me again, you'd better do it quick before we have to sit down and explain all this to him."

He passed a gentle hand over her hair. "I don't know what kind of family we're going to make, Claudia, but we're going to do our damnedest to make it as close to our dreams as possible."

"That's all I want. You're all I want."

"Same goes, babe. Now lay one on me so we can go back to all those people spying on us from down the street and tell them the news."

"What news is that?" Claudia asked coyly.

"The news that you're finally going to make an honest man out of me."

She laughed, and it was music to his ears and his heart.

****

That night, Claudia and Nate sat Justin down in the living room above Decadence. Claudia asked Zoe to find something else to do so that she, Nate, and Justin could talk together as the family she hoped they would soon be.

"What's up, guys?" Justin said, coming into the living room with his ball and mitt in his hands. "Is Nate going to take me to the batting cages? That would be really cool." He slyly looked at Nate out of the corner of his eye, and Claudia couldn't tell if Justin was just trying to get one over on them or if someone had told him about the display in front of Decadence before she got a chance to lay it out for him herself.

Nate laughed and held Claudia's hand. Justin's eyes zeroed in on the motion in a split second. His face squinched up, and Claudia wasn't sure if he was about to cry or cheer.

"Justin, Nate and I would like to talk to you."

"Why is he holding your hand? I've seen him hold your hand to help you over a short fence or something, but not just hold your hand when you're sitting down." He looked skeptical, and she couldn't blame him.

"Well, honey, this is what we wanted to talk to you

about." Claudia cleared her throat, not sure where to actually go with the conversation now that she had started it. "Um…"

Nate jumped in. "Look, guy, what your mom is trying to say is that…um…"

She and Nate both laughed, looking at each other. They weren't going to be able to wade slowly into this. "Nate and I are dating," Claudia blurted out, hoping it wouldn't rock Justin's world in a bad way. As happy as she'd been to tell Nate she loved him today, she'd also feared what it would do to Justin. But she couldn't ignore her heart anymore.

"Cool." Justin sat back against the chair and smiled at both of them.

"Just cool? You don't have anything else to say?" Claudia peered at him closely to make sure he wasn't hiding his real feelings. She glanced at Nate, who was doing the same thing.

"Yep, just cool."

"Okay," Nate said, then kissed the back of Claudia's hand. Was he testing the waters?

Justin laughed, right before he groaned. "Oh, man, I'm not going to have to watch you guys be all lovey-dovey and stuff, am I? I told Grandma when she said she wanted the two of you to get together that I didn't know if I'd be able to handle that. I guess it's okay, though, as long as I don't have to watch too much smooching."

Claudia burst out laughing, and so did Nate. "Did you just say that you and Grandma orchestrated this whole thing?"

"I don't think I'd use that big of a word, but sure." Justin grinned at them. "She told me all about her plan to introduce you to all those stupid guys so you might see what was right in front of you. I didn't know what she meant at first, but then she said Nate. At first I thought it would be gross, because Nate's like my best friend. But then I thought about it some more, and the more I thought about it the cooler it got. Who else gets to have their best friend living in their house all the time and making their mom happy? It's going to be so cool! Don't date too long, though," he said, looking at them both head-on. "I want to be able to call him Dad and live in his house with all those flat screen TVs real soon!"

And then he threw down his ball and mitt and jumped onto the couch with them, screaming about how happy he was.

Claudia sat shell-shocked for a moment before being dragged into the first family hug of many. Life was good and would hopefully only get better.

****

Hours later, with Justin finally in bed and Zoe home for the night, Claudia felt like a schoolgirl, sneaking over to Nate's house. She was going to have her cake and eat it too, and she was going to do it tonight. Zoe had shooed her out of the house without even a farewell, telling her to get her groove on and not to look back.

She hadn't had sex in so many years, it hurt her girl parts to think about it, but she had dressed the part under her blouse and capris and hoped Nate would love it. The tiny, pink, silky panties perfectly matched the push-up bra clinging to her boobs. She'd shaved, waxed and lotioned to her heart's content.

Yes, this could be a huge mistake. Yes, it could

ruin her friendship of many years with a man who meant the world to her. But it could also enhance it a thousandfold. Nights with Nate wrapped around her like gift wrap, days of sharing with him across the kitchen table, snatching kisses and quick caresses when Justin wasn't looking. This was her chance at making the family she'd always wanted, and with a man who made her heart sing a song like never before.

Of course, she still had doubts and anxieties about the whole thing. Nothing in life was a sure bet. Even making a cake while following the recipe to the last letter didn't always produce the same result every single time. But you had to try before you could fail. And that was just what she was going to do tonight and hopefully for the rest of her life. She was going to grab this chance with Nate, the chance she thought she'd never have or want again, and run with it as far as possible.

Her hands were sweaty on the wheel of her car when she pulled up in front of his house. God, what if she had forgotten how to have sex?

But when Nate opened the front door and barely let her all the way into the foyer before giving her the first orgasm of the night, with his hands in her pants and his tongue doing wicked, wicked things to her neck and earlobe, she knew her fears were ridiculous.

It was the first of many, and she returned the favor over and over again throughout the night. It was only as dawn peeked in through the upstairs curtains that she fell into an exhausted sleep. As she hovered between this world and dreamland, she had a vision of herself at Decadence in the coming months.

Tears would be going around even before it was

time to see the dress May would make over bowls of cornflakes and endless reruns of old shows. The wave of laughter and tears would come, and when it did, Mona would have control of the volume and intensity. When it quieted and when it swelled. The flowers would be made by her sister from the loveliest blooms.

And her cake would have sprinkles, and be made with the finest sugar.

A word about the author...

Misty Simon lives in Central Pennsylvania and is happiest when she is creating stories that make you laugh out loud. Everyone needs some laughter in their lives and she is all too happy to provide.

You can find her on the web at:
www.mistysimon.com.